Objects
in Mirror

5 4 3 2 1

Published in Canada by Red Deer Press
195 Allstate Parkway, Markham, ON, L3R 4T8

www.reddeerpress.com

Published in the United States by Red Deer Press
311 Washington Street, Brighton, Massachusetts, 02135

Cover and text design by Daniel Choi
Cover image courtesy of Shelly J. F. Hoyles

We acknowledge with thanks the Canada Council for the Arts, and the Ontario Arts Council for their support of our publishing program. We acknowledge the financial support of the Government of Canada through the Canada Book Fund (CBF) for our publishing activities.

ONTARIO ARTS COUNCIL
CONSEIL DES ARTS DE L'ONTARIO
50 YEARS OF ONTARIO GOVERNMENT SUPPORT OF THE ARTS
50 ANS DE SOUTIEN DU GOUVERNEMENT DE L'ONTARIO AUX ARTS

**Canada Council
for the Arts**

**Conseil des Arts
du Canada**

Library and Archives Canada Cataloguing in Publication
Roberts, Tudor
    Objects in mirror / Tudor Robins.
ISBN 978-0-88995-497-7
    I. Title.
PS8635.O2275O25 2013   jC813'.6   C2013-901671-6

Publisher Cataloging-in-Publication Data (U.S.)
Robins, Tudor.
    Objects in mirror / Tudor Robins.
[224] p. : cm.
Summary: A teenager finds her dream summer job working with horses. What make the job even better are her handsome co-worker and a fragile, damaged mare that needs extra care. But the eating disorder she is starting to acknowledge but not truly understand rears its head, and she must find out if she can heal herself along with the horses she is caring for.
ISBN-13: 978-0-88995-497-7 (pbk.)
1. Horses – Juvenile fiction. 3. Eating disorders in adolescence – Juvenile fiction. I. Title
[Fic] dc23   PZ7.R6356Ob 2013

MIX
Paper from
responsible sources
FSC® C103113
www.fsc.org

Printed and bound in Canada

Objects *in* Mirror

Tudor Robins

Red Deer Press

For Bryn, Evan, and Tim,
who inspire, motivate, and support.

chapter

one

The whipper-in calls my number—"Seventy-two, you're on deck!"—and, as though he understands that's us, Sprite dances sideways, nearly slamming the clipboard-wielding gentleman into the white fence boards.

This is the big class of the day. I'm as excited as Sprite, but one of us has to stay calm. Serenity doesn't come naturally to hepped-up off-the-track thoroughbreds like Sprite. Which leaves me to be the sensible one.

I sink my heels deeper in my stirrups, settle my seat more firmly into the saddle, and point my thumbs up.

Back straight, big smile, look cool, and send Sprite, in his beautiful sweeping trot, into the ring.

Where he promptly grabs the bit, yanks his head down, and lets his back heels fly.

Sprite wants to jump. Sprite sees no need to bend or flex, to circle or warm up. He enters the ring with his eyes and ears flicking from jump to jump.

In Sprite's mind, all I'm good for is pointing him at the first obstacle, after which I should back off and stop bugging him so he can finish the course.

I've ridden horses that can autopilot courses. Some of my competitors own horses like that. Sprite, however, is not one of those horses. Given his head, Sprite would jump everything twice, then get bored and jump the fence out of the ring, to keep on running and jumping everything in his path.

I know this because I've seen him do it.

So I give him a firm half-halt as I smile wider than ever, mutter "bugger" under my breath, and step him into the forward canter we need for our approach to the first fence.

He clears it by eighteen inches, and jump two, as well. He leaves at least two feet between his belly and the top rail of jump three and throws in a tail flourish on the landing. *Here we go.*

Sure enough, as he rounds the far corner, Sprite throws out a lightning-fast series of bucks. There are always three in quick succession, and those trademark three bucks will leave me only four or five precious strides to set him up for the diagonal combination.

"Excuse me!" I use my seat and my legs and my hands

and my voice, too—a horse like Sprite requires every aid in the box—and we battle our way over the three increasingly wide jumps. By the end of the line, he's flying, reaching, digging, and the sturdy white ring fence is coming faster and faster, and we need to turn the corner in enough control to get over the tall vertical propped on the short end.

"Listen!" I tell him, but it's a tool for me, too, reminding me first and foremost to get it done. Forget pretty, forget elegant; those can come later if we make the flat phase but for now, my priorities are (1) don't knock down any jumps, (2) don't die.

We dig in deep to the base of the vertical and, with a super-athletic effort, Sprite twists himself over it without bringing the rail down. To celebrate, he indulges in his biggest buck yet.

Despite the noise and activity of the show grounds, all I can hear is my own voice ordering Sprite to "Smarten up!" then Drew's yelling, "Go, girl!"

"Go!" I tell Sprite. *Go, go, go*, and, with that, we're not fighting any more. We're four jumps from being home and we want the same thing—to get over them fast and clean—I lean forward, give Sprite a nudge, and soften my hands.

The new gear he clicks into is so fast it's almost scary. I hardly have time to breathe, as Sprite pins his ears back against his neck, throws all his energy forward, and jumps the jumps.

When he's not in mid-air, he's running flat-out, and when he clears the last jump, I have to keep him galloping around the ring because there's no way I can stop him in time for a polite exit from the gate.

Fantastic, amazing, exhilarating, unbelievable. I'm hooked, hooked, hooked. Want to go right back in and do it again. Want to jump like that all summer long.

"Pinch me!" I tell Drew as I ride out of the ring, because I can't believe Sprite's mine for the season and I *do* get to do this all summer long.

"Don't relax yet," Drew tells me. "You're through to the flat. Now you've got to make him behave."

♦ ♦ ♦

Four days later, my Sprite-induced jumping high hasn't worn off. It doesn't hurt that we placed third; an amazing showing, considering Sprite had to suffer through the flat portion of the class.

It's not like school's been distracting me. With the temperature hitting twenty-eight by fourth period, even the teachers are more focused on beaches and cottages than learning objectives and curriculum.

When I get on the school bus for my final ride of the year, and settle my butt onto the ripped vinyl of my usual seat, I have nothing left to think about—nothing to plan for, study for, or worry about—other than riding, and showing, and Sprite. I drift into a play-by-play rerun of our weekend jumping round so vivid that half my brain's still back at the show grounds as I step off the bus at the end of our gravel country driveway.

Only to be rugby-tackled around the knees.

"Ooof!" I yell. My arms flail for something, anything, to break my fall. Finding nothing, I go down hard, hitting the ground with a thump, swiftly followed by the second thump of my backpack full of books, bouncing off the gravel to hit me on the head.

"I'm Sowwy, Gwacie!" It's Jamie, my three-year-old brother, straddling my waist.

"I might believe you if you didn't look so happy," I tell him.

"Come on, you; give Grace some peace." Annabelle says, hauling him off, then holding out her hand to help me up. "He's so excited to see you. He can't stop talking about how you're going to be around all summer long."

Jamie runs off ahead of us, weaving from side to side across the driveway, stopping every now and then to make a wild jump in the air or kick out at his shadow. He reminds me of Sprite but without the bad nature.

"He insisted we make lemonade for you." Annabelle's trying, just that little bit too hard, to keep her voice light and easy. How can one simple sentence be so loaded, mean so much more than the sum of its words?

"Good," I say. "I'm hot." And Annabelle smiles. I've said the right thing: *I'll have some*, just not in so many words.

She takes my hand and, even though I'm nearly sixteen and, even though she's my stepmom, I let her. Even squeeze back a bit and, actually, it feels quite nice.

chapter

two

I hose Sprite down in the outdoor wash stall. *With this horse I can go places.* He's pretty, even soaking wet. In the next wash stall over, Mavis, who rides in my lesson and shows with me, is bathing her horse, Ava. Despite the rumored huge sum Mavis's parents paid for her, Ava looks more like a miserable drowned rat than a championship hunter-jumper.

The uncharitable thought about Ava clears my mind in a flash. But a flash of distraction is all Sprite needs. His ears pin back, head snakes forward, and he reaches big ugly teeth for Ava's dripping neck.

His halter-tie stops him just inches from his target, and he shakes his head and stamps his feet in frustration.

"Why'd you have to lease the world's meanest horse?" Mavis asks.

Why'd you have to buy the world's stupidest? I want to fire back because, seriously, what kind of dumb horse would doze off the way Ava's doing when Sprite's threatening teeth are so close?

I keep quiet, though, because my mean horse is also gorgeous and talented. He's breathtaking to ride, unlike meek and mild Ava, and he's going to win me the championships Mavis has had pretty much all to herself up until now. That's payback enough.

I'm so sick of Mavis having an edge on me. She was the first in our lesson to get her own pony and, after winning all she could on him, her parents were happy to keep upgrading her horses. Ava—trailered in from Virginia— is the latest and most expensive in a long chain of push-button, championship-winning machines, keeping Mavis festooned in ribbons and lugging trophies home from almost every show.

Mavis lords her wealth over me every chance she gets. Her dad is some high-up exec in the local NHL team, so she has box tickets to every event held at the arena, in addition to an endless stream of new designer clothes and fancy riding gear.

Even though those aren't the kinds of things I want, I do wish things didn't come so easily to Mavis. Her nickname (behind her back only) is "hipbones," earned the time she showed everyone in the lesson how she could pull her breeches right off without undoing them. "These are the ones I bought last year that were so tight, you could read the date on a dime through them," she said. "I can't believe I was ever that huge." At this, she sent meaningful glances around the tack room, lingering on girls who'd have a hard time fitting into her breeches at all, let alone pulling them down over their hips.

Things like that make me hate Mavis, but I hate myself more for listening, giving her an audience.

Mavis wants a rise out of me now and pushes me harder. "How can you stand having the evil stepmother riding here?"

She waves toward the sand ring where Annabelle's taking her weekly lesson with Drew.

Annabelle listens attentively to something Drew says, and her hand weaves through the air to trace an imaginary path over the jumps he's telling her to take. She nods, picks up her reins, and is off. Nails it. Gets all her distances right first try.

If Annabelle really was an evil stepmother, things like that would make it pretty easy to hate her. But since Mavis missed the mark there, too, I stay resolutely silent; scrub at a manure stain on Sprite's hock, all the while making sure he doesn't take a chunk out of my backside.

"Seriously, Grace," Mavis pushes on. "Doesn't it kill you that not only is she skinnier and prettier than you, but she also rides better than you ever will?"

"Thanks for the compliments." I avoid meeting Mavis's

eyes as I sponge away the soap and watch the manure stain disappear with the suds.

"At least my mom's normal," Mavis says. "She's annoying, she can't ride, and she's fat. That's how moms should be."

I mist Sprite one last time to make sure he's squeaky clean, then snap the lead shank onto his halter and untie him from the wash stall.

"Well, you know what they say about mothers and daughters, Mavis. If you want to see how a girl will turn out in twenty-five years, just look at her mother."

And I take my ill-tempered horse away to graze and dry off, while I watch the rest of my not-so-wicked stepmother's ride.

chapter

three

After our Tuesday evening lesson, Drew asks me to stay behind. The satisfaction that always tingles through my brain and body at the end of a hard lesson, loosening my muscles and letting my mind wander, flees. I tense, and Sprite jumps sideways, into the path of one of the other girls in my lesson who's too nice to tell me off, but probably should.

Drew's summons of me—just me—is rare in the extreme. He mostly treats his students as a homogeneous group: teenage girls on horseback. The closest any of us comes to getting individual attention is if he happens to use our name when he yells at one of us. At the end of our allotted hour, we chorus an obligatory round of "Thank you, Drew," and he waves his hand to show we're collectively dismissed.

Mavis raises her eyebrows at me, and I turn Sprite back toward Drew's podium at the center of the ring. I mimic Mavis and raise my own eyebrows, as I draw Sprite to a halt beside Drew.

"There's something I need to tell you," he says. The bottom of my stomach twitches. It's preparing to bail on me, to drop away and leave me sick and shaky. "There's no easy way to say this, and I'm very sorry, but you're not going to be able to show Sprite at Cedar Mills this weekend."

The fear of transgressing a stable rule always lives in the back of my mind. I'm paranoid I'll turn my horse out with the wrong boots on, or forget to clean my bit when I put my bridle away. Drew's "sorry" tells me I'm not the one in trouble. I'm still on edge, but at least I'm able to find my voice.

Like all Drew's students, I'm conditioned to be polite at all times. He's sent riders out of the ring at the beginning of a fifty-dollar lesson for muttering under their breath. He tells their parents no, they will not be getting a refund. So, while I think, *What are you talking about?*, what I say is, "Pardon me?"

"Sprite's been sold, Grace."

My intestines twist. My breath goes.

I lock my eyes on the distant maple I used as my focal point while we were jumping just a few minutes ago. *If you stare at the tree, everything will be OK.*

"Grace?" Drew's voice contains uncharacteristic kindness. He knows me so well; can tell my outside leg is two inches too far back, even when he's watching me from the inside of the ring. I bite my lip and swat an imaginary fly from the far side of Sprite's neck. Of course, Drew probably knows there was no fly there.

"Grace, it's terrible timing, but we couldn't say no. Sprite's not much use to us. After all, you're the only one who can ride him." This is high praise indeed—the highest I'll probably ever get from Drew—and I can't even enjoy it.

"When we got the offer, we had to take it. Buyers for horses this tough don't come along every day."

I press my fingers across my lips and point at Sprite's steaming neck, then up at the barn.

"You're right," Drew says. "Take him up and sponge him down, and we'll talk about it more before you leave. There are a few possibilities we should discuss."

"Your dinner's ready!" I ignore Annabelle as I struggle to remove my half-chaps—*stupid zippers!*—and yank my paddock boots off—*dumb laces!*

Catch a glimpse of myself in the full-length mirror hanging on the near side of the powder room door. *Great, are my ankles getting fat now, too?* I've always hated these socks. I yank them off inside out and whip the resulting balls at the mirror.

"Grace?"

"Leave me alone." It's not loud enough for her to hear, but it feels rebellious anyway.

"I said ..." Her voice is getting closer. She's heading to the mud room to find me.

I am *so* not ready to have a dinner discussion with Annabelle right now. I haven't rehearsed my response, what with Drew's announcement's throwing me so completely off my stride.

"I'm going for a run!" I grab a pair of dirty running shorts from the laundry basket sitting on the washing machine. They stink and I'll stink wearing them, but who cares?

"Grace!" There's a hint of what we jokingly call "young lady" in Annabelle's voice. When I'm coming close to the edge of acceptable behavior, she'll wag her finger at me and warn, "Young lady..." It's usually enough to diffuse a tense situation but, this time, I'm not laughing.

"I'm going running!" I leave my dusty boots and half-chaps skewed across the floor—just the way Annabelle hates them. My discarded breeches catch in the door as I try to slam it behind me. Another gift for Annabelle.

Screw her. Screw everything. Screw Sprite's new owner. Screw Mavis, who has her own horse and spends all her time bitching she wants a better one. Screw my dad— not for leaving us—but for being too self-absorbed to listen when I told him how much I wanted Sprite, when I offered to pay for half his sale price. Screw my screwed-up life.

No horse has ever given me the feeling I get on Sprite. No

horse has ever let me ride so close to the brink of control while trusting him, every time and always, to get the job done. The reason I can ride Sprite when nobody else can, is we're wired the same. I don't try to hold him back at every step and he respects me for it. Together we fly.

I thought I had a whole summer of that experience ahead of me. Had desperately hoped somehow we'd win enough prize money, or my dad would relent, and I'd be able to buy Sprite after all. Now, that can never happen. My throat aches.

My only hope is to run this feeling out of my system, to exhaust myself. To keep pushing until I'm too tired to be angry. To cry from exertion instead of despair. It's getting dark but I need to do this. I can run in the dark. What's the big deal?

Except I haven't gone far before my route leads through a stand of trees, their canopy so thick it blocks out all remaining daylight. I twist my ankle and mutter, "Shit." Then yell it. "Shit!" It doesn't help, though, because a swarm of mosquitoes is circling and, in the short space of time I'm standing still, they fly into my ears and my nostrils and raise bites on my exposed arms.

"Aaaarrrggghhh!!!!" Boiling with frustration, I turn for home.

I brush past Annabelle in the hallway and stomp up the stairs to the shower. I don't dare repeat my foul language there—Jamie would pick it up in no time flat and be expelled from playgroup—but I bang things around and do a satisfactory bit of sighing and grunting, just to make sure my annoyance is clear.

I crank the hot water so it stings the places that are always sore after I ride. The patch of skin just inside my right shinbone that rubs raw no matter what socks I wear. The tender crease between my fingers where Sprite's new cheap canvas reins wreak havoc. I wonder if his new rider will buy him better reins. Wonder if she'll buy a whole new bridle.

I wonder if Annabelle knew. That's the worst of it. Annabelle, who I can always talk to. Annabelle, who knows how much I wanted to show Sprite. Annabelle, whose best friend is Drew's wife, Andy. She must have known. She couldn't have. She had to …

I dry myself in the hall so I don't have to look in the mirror. The last thing I need right now is to count one fewer rib tonight than I did this time yesterday.

When I come back downstairs, I'm cleaner but feel no better.

"Good lesson?" Annabelle lifts one eyebrow.

I stare at her.

"Do you want to tell me what's up?"

"I'm not sure. It depends."

"Depends on what?"

"Depends on whether you already knew."

"About?" She looks genuinely curious. It diffuses my anger, but just a bit.

"About me not showing this weekend. Or, as far as I know, any weekend at all. About Sprite being sold. About my entire summer—probably my entire life—being *ruined*."

"Oh, Gracie!" She gasps. "Not Sprite!" Her eyes redden and her hand flies to cover her mouth.

I open my mouth to go on. To tell her how it's always been twice as hard for me to keep up with all the other kids who have their own horses; and how I have to be three times as good a rider to get half the results; and how this year I really, really had a chance to do great things. But the thing is, she already knows. She backed me up when I lobbied my dad to buy Sprite, and she used those exact arguments.

I gulp for breath and tears spill down my cheeks, and I'm even getting a little snotty. But, to her credit, and even though she's wearing a clean and very pretty shirt, Annabelle gives me a hug.

She guides me to a chair, where I sit down and blubber some more and sob out, "Nobody understands ..." and "It's not fair ..." and, out of the blue, a small body launches into my lap.

Jamie, bathed and in pyjamas, ready for bed. Warm and rosy and smelling wonderful. His arms go around me. "Oh, Jamesy-boy," I say. "Thanks, that makes me feel better."

Except his face is turning red, too, and he's not hugging me; he's grabbing me, pulling frantically at me. And he's shrieking louder than any of my sobs, "GWACIE! YOU ARE SITTING ON SNIFFLES! GET OFF HIM!"

I reach behind me and encounter the purple squishiness of Jamie's precious T-Rex shoved between my backside and the chair back. I pull him out, hand him to Jamie, and turn to Annabelle.

"Nothing like a real problem to put you in your place." I even manage to smile a bit while I say it.

Annabelle laughs and laughs. She laughs so hard, her eyes water, joining Jamie's and my tearful ranks.

"I love both of you," she says. "You have no idea." Then she wipes the tears from her cheeks, grabs Jamie's hand, swings Sniffles from the other, and takes them both upstairs to bed.

I sit for a few minutes, soaking in the calm after the evening's storm, when, interrupting the quiet, the phone rings.

It takes me a few seconds to place the voice on the line. It's intensely familiar but I can't remember ever hearing it on the phone.

"Drew?"

"None other."

"Why are you calling?"

"We were supposed to talk. You left."

"I, uh, had to get home."

"You were pissed off, more like," he says.

I sigh, walk over to my favorite chair, fold myself into it. "Upset, maybe," I admit. "I wouldn't say pissed off."

Drew's charisma loses nothing by being filtered through the phone line. He chuckles as he says, "No, I guess you wouldn't. Annabelle would kill you." I didn't plan to soften tonight, but it's happening. My tense shoulders drop in response to Drew's familiar charm. It's hard to stay angry when he turns on his magnetism.

As if magicked up by Drew's mention of her, Annabelle enters the room. *Who is it?* she mouths.

Drew, I mouth back. Her eyebrows arch and she crosses the room, gives my arm a quick squeeze before pointing to the doorway to the kitchen. *I'll be right in there.*

I don't answer because Drew's talking again.

"I have two options for you." The flip side of Drew's dynamism is his impatience. I'd better pay attention.

"We promised you a horse to show, and you've paid in advance for the whole summer, so we owe you a horse to show." I can't argue with Drew's logic. It's just that I can't imagine what horse he has to offer me.

He takes a deep breath. Lets drama build for a few quiet seconds. "So, Andy and I are prepared to bring Serendipity out of retirement and offer her to you."

Whoa. I didn't see that one coming. Serendipity is my mental image of a picture-perfect hunter-jumper mare come to life. She's sixteen-one. Bay with white points. Perfectly proportioned. Trained to the eyeballs. A multi-show, multi-year A-circuit champion. She glides on the flat and she floats over jumps. I wouldn't have space on my walls for the ribbons I'd win on her.

She's a dream. *But she's not yours.* The thought zings into my brain, but I don't have time to dwell on it. There's mounting impatience in Drew's voice.

"Grace? Are you there?" Protracted silence is clearly not the reaction he was expecting.

"Um, yes. Sorry. That's an amazing offer. I'm a bit shocked, actually."

Annabelle's head appears around the door frame. *What?*

"Serendipity," I say into the phone for her benefit. "Wow!"

Annabelle claps her hand to her mouth, drops the tea towel she's holding.

I look away from her so I can focus on what Drew's saying. "Yes, well, she's fit and she seems to still be enjoying the work. Of course, you couldn't do jumper on her, and the over-fences hunter classes would have to be low, but, conditional on her health, we'd be happy to have you show her."

"I see."

"However ..."

Oh, of course, a catch. I knew there'd be a catch. "Uh-huh," I say. *Lay it on me.* I've already lost my chance to ride one horse tonight. Might as well kick me while I'm down.

"Andy and I wanted to give you an alternative option."

"Like, in addition to the Serendipity option?"

"Of course." I'm annoying him. If he was a horse, he'd be stamping his hoof, scraping the barn floor.

"OK. I'm listening."

"We need help."

"Help?"

"We're busier than we've ever been before. We have riders showing three circuits this summer. Karen can't work seven days a week." I picture wiry little Karen, scuttling down from her studio apartment over the stables, finding work to be done anywhere but where people are. She loves horses but doesn't ride, isn't great with customers and, as Drew says, can't work all the time.

"We need someone to work alongside Matt this summer. Someone who can school horses, show them to buyers, exercise them when the owners are away."

Matt. One year ahead of me at school and light years ahead of me with horses.

Matt the horse god. Not even a horse whisperer—stronger than that. Matt, who can ride any horse over any obstacle, with each element of his position intact and a smile on his face.

Drew and I both know I am *not* in Matt's league.

So I test him. "You mean someone who can muck out stalls?"

"Sometimes," Drew says. "The basics have to be done, but that's not the main job."

This decision should be a no-brainer. I should be saying, "Thanks, I'll be over to ride Serendipity tomorrow." But I'm not. I'm teetering. And while I'm teetering, Drew says the thing that gives me a great big nudge.

"Sprite's staying here."

"What?" The word jumps out of me before Annabelle's years of training in good manners kick in. "Sorry, pardon?"

"His new owner's going to need help with him. She's

fairly inexperienced. She's leaving him with us and paying to have him schooled ..."

"And you're offering to pay me to school him?" *I might not have lost Sprite.*

"That's right."

"Any chance that would include showing him?"

Drew sighs. For the first time in the conversation, there's patience in his voice. "I'd like to say yes, Grace. And I'm not going to say it's a categorical no. But it is unlikely. They bought him for her to show him."

Never mind who gets him ready for those shows. I don't say it out loud, though. Just because it's not my style doesn't change the fact that lots of people show horses other people have trained.

Having said what he called to say, Drew's done with the conversation. "Listen, Grace, I know it's not exactly what you wanted, but it might be better. You'd be getting paid to ride Sprite during the week, and there would probably be other opportunities for you to show. Andy and I both hope you'll take us up on this offer. We could use you."

"Can I tell you tomorrow?" My head's spinning. I need to talk to Annabelle. To sleep on it. To think.

"Tell us when you're ready." It's the last thing I hear before the "click," telling me Drew's off to tackle some other task on his to-do list.

I carry the receiver back to its cradle in the kitchen. My tiny contribution to putting the house back in order before bedtime.

Annabelle's been busy. The counters are clear; the sink gleams. She folds the tea towel in thirds, threads it through the handle on the oven, and says, "Well?"

"Well, I have a big decision to make."

"You wanna come up and talk to me about it while I fold laundry?"

"Sounds good." I flick the switch nearest me to cut the under-cabinet lighting. Annabelle turns off the pot lights over the sink.

Made it. She's forgotten about my dinner. No need for excuses that I'm full, or lies about someone ordering pizza at the barn. A thrill of satisfaction runs through me.

I'll be home-free as long as my stomach doesn't set up a long and protracted growl while we talk about Drew's phone call. Too bad folding laundry isn't a noisier occupation.

Journal - Tuesday, July 2

▷ 21.9 lbs down from start weight.

▷ 5k run (too short: bugs, dark), 60 sit-ups.

▷ Can't face the bulge of my stomach every time I walk in my room
  —maybe hang a towel over my mirror?

Food highlight: Missed dinner and no conflict. Bonus.

Food lowlight: Life lowlight is losing show season on Sprite. No food lowlight today.

Calorie intake: approx. 1000 (No dinner helps …).

chapter

four

I sneeze and the flashlight dips.

"Hey!" Annabelle protests. "Light!"

"Sorry." I point the beam back at the gloomy spot where I last saw Annabelle's back, and brace myself for my inevitable two follow-up sneezes. I always sneeze three times in a row and Jamie does, too. It's a trait inherited from my—*our*—dad. When he lived here, and one of us would triple-sneeze, Annabelle would always shake her head and say, "There go those weird Madden genes again. Glad I don't have them."

"Ta-da!" She reappears from the depths of the furnace room, and her flushed cheeks and sparkling eyes ensure she's as pretty as ever, despite the dishevelment of her hair and the cobweb clinging to her right shoulder. "I found them!"

"They'll never fit. They'll be way too small." I've been saying this ever since Annabelle offered me the use of her old chaps. Ever since I shared my worry that I wouldn't know what to wear if I took the job Drew offered.

"Of course they'll fit." Annabelle's said this half-a-dozen times. "They'll be perfect. On really hot days, you can wear shorts and then just put these on when you need to ride."

"They'll be perfect *if* they fit," I mutter.

"Oh, shut up and go upstairs." There's the first hint of true annoyance in Annabelle's voice, and she never says "shut up" so, instead of pushing my luck, I switch off the flashlight and head up the basement stairs.

"They fit!" There's more than a hint of "I told you so" in Annabelle's voice. "In fact, I'll need to lace them tighter." She slips two fingers into the back strap to demonstrate the space there. "How do they feel?"

I bend my knees, crouch low, stand back up, turn from side to side. "They're really comfy. I'm amazed. I never thought they'd ..."

"Fit? Really? You weren't sure? Grace, you have a truly distorted idea of how big you are."

We're perilously close to a conversation I don't want to have. I deflect her. "It's just that you're so tall."

"Freakishly tall, you mean?"

My jaw drops. "Oh, my God, Annabelle. How can you say

that about yourself? You're gorgeously tall."

Her slow nod and narrowed eyes tell me I've walked right into her trap. "Just goes to show, people have weird ideas about the way they look, don't they, Grace?"

My tongue twitches with the desire to talk back. But I'm getting better at thinking before I speak. *Do you really want to piss off the one adult who's actually stuck around with you?*

Good point. I keep quiet.

"Now, it probably wouldn't hurt to just trim an inch or so off the bottom. Stay here while I find the scissors ..."

One leg's done, and I'm waiting for her to start in on the other one, when Annabelle sits back on her heels, clears her throat, and hovers the open scissors absentmindedly by her ear.

Maybe it's just the splayed blades so close to her fabulously shiny long hair, but a stab of tension runs through me, turns my core to Jell-O.

Is she going to say something? Is she going to keep trimming? I shift my weight, breathe in through my nose, and open my mouth to say something, anything to break the loaded silence, when she speaks.

"The job is great. And I want you to take it." In the pause that follows, I know I wasn't imagining the tension. "But Thursdays are not negotiable."

Aaah, *Thursdays*. I should have known everything was going too well.

Keep calm. Be reasonable. Don't whine. "Why?" *Oh, God, I'm whining already.* "I hate Dr. Keelor. She's useless. I don't need her."

"You promised." Those two words should be enough to win the argument. Still, Annabelle holds her breath. She lays the scissors—still open—down beside her and crosses her arms tightly.

She's right. I did promise. I promised because driving to the other side of Ottawa every Thursday morning to meet Dr. Keelor didn't seem so bad when it meant missing school. I promised because of the night I'd crept downstairs to hear Annabelle crying on the phone, saying, "I'm afraid she's going to die. I don't know what to do with her." That had sent a bolt of cold, blue fear straight through me, reminding me of the last months and weeks with my dad, who had more than once yelled, "I don't know what to do with you!" at both Jamie and me.

A tiny part of me also promised because I was tired. The initial elation of losing ten pounds, and then twenty— of dropping down two breeches sizes—had worn off. I'd entered the battle zone, where every pound was a fight. Successes came slowly, and defeats were no longer a fat hunk of cheesecake away; instead, a slice of regular bread, no butter, could spell disaster. There were moments where it was clear as day that the control I originally thought I'd achieved was gone, and the tables were turned. I no longer called the shots; I just tried to dodge them. Some help might be nice.

But Dr. Keelor is no help. And now, visiting her each week will mean giving up a precious morning at the barn. I want to kick up a fuss. To stamp my feet. To refuse. But *Annabelle*. Annabelle, crouching in front of me, biting her lip. Annabelle, not knowing what to do with me.

"OK." A twinge of guilt tickles me at the relief on Annabelle's face. The relaxing of her arms, her humming as she picks up the scissors again. She's so happy, but I've promised so little. Almost nothing, really.

I'll go to Dr. Keelor's every week, and it will cost Annabelle time, and gas, and the exorbitant parking fees they charge at the children's hospital, but that doesn't mean I'll *do* anything. Doesn't mean I'll *change*. I know how to sit in an office and nod, and if that's what I have to keep doing once a week for the foreseeable future, to keep Annabelle happy, that's what I'll do.

◆ ◆ ◆

I clear my throat, then stop. Is that rude? Should I even be in here while Drew's talking on the phone? Maybe I should wait out in the aisle. But I was already in the office—really a converted box stall across from the tack room, tarted up with curtains and containing a desk—when Drew answered the phone, so it must be OK.

Tap, tap, tap. I flick my dressage whip against the side of my paddock boot. *Tap, tap, tap.* Drew cocks one eyebrow, stares at my foot. *Crap!* Must. Stop. Fidgeting. Lean the whip against the door frame, where it promptly falls over, whacking the side of the metal wastepaper bin. *Double crap.*

"The farrier's in tomorrow. I can't say anything before I get his opinion." I'm relieved to hear impatience tingeing Drew's voice as he talks to somebody else: a client. *It's not just me.* "No, don't call me; I'll call you when I know something. Goodbye." He beeps the call to an end and I picture a baffled horse owner standing in her kitchen, staring at her suddenly dead phone.

"Well?" Drew's scribbling something on a piece of paper, so I'm not positive he's talking to me. Until he raises his voice. "Come on, Grace, what is it? Do you have an answer for me?"

Nice day. Beautiful sunshine. Not a cloud in the sky. No small talk with Drew. "Yes."

"And?" I swear he's going to snap his fingers any minute.

"Yes." I say again. If he doesn't want to waste time, we don't have to.

He snaps his fingers. *What am I? A dog?* I bite the words back. "That's it?" he says. "Yes?"

"Yes, please. I'd like to work for you. I think it's a great opportunity."

"You don't want Serendipity?"

Oh, such a loaded question. Since he made it clear last night he thought I should take the job, it's obviously a test. How to pass?

Several too-long and convoluted answers form in my head. I lose interest before I can get them out. Drew would never let me finish them. *Keep it short.* "I want a challenge."

His face splits in a beaming smile. Ah, the charisma again! Basking in its glow is like nothing else in the world. He takes two steps across the office and grabs me in a bear hug. "That's my girl!" I *am* his girl. The smartest girl in the world. I'm great. Drew loves me. I'm a star.

For the five seconds that pass before I say, "There's just one thing."

He pulls back, his eyebrows knit together; the sunbeam smile inverts. "What one thing?"

"Thursdays. Annabelle wanted me to say I can't work Thursday mornings." Will he ask why? Will we have to talk about it?

I cross and uncross my fingers as I wait for his reaction. If my fingers are crossed when he speaks, it'll be OK. If he catches them uncrossed, the Thursdays will be a deal breaker. Cross, uncross. Cross, uncross. Drew covers the short space back to his desk, spreads his hands across the planner lying there. Makes another scribbled note. I wait.

His eyes meet mine and I hurry to cross my fingers.

"I don't see a problem with that. You can be here in the afternoons?"

I nod. "By one, at the latest."

He taps the page with the pencil before dropping it into the dip formed by the binding. "Done. Since tomorrow's Thursday, do you want to start Friday? Make your first day a whole one?"

"Done." My echo of his word earns me a sideways glance,

but the phone rings and he waves his hand to dismiss me.

The words "Friday at 8:30!" follow me out the door. Then, "Stonegate Farms, Drew speaking."

I got away with it. Why do I feel that way? Because I know Andy knows about Thursday mornings. I know because, more than once, we've dropped Jamie off here on our way into the city, and Andy's given Annabelle's hand a squeeze and said, "Good luck. Don't worry about him." And I also know Drew's not one to have his wife busy looking after someone else's child without knowing why.

Truth be told, I've been waiting for weeks now—for months—for Drew to pull me aside. To give me a lecture about losing weight too quickly and jeopardizing my health and, therefore, my riding. When he called me over in our lesson last night, I was dreading just that conversation. But despite regularly telling riders off for gaining too much weight, and even though he ordered a girl I used to ride with to stop seeing her drug-dealing boyfriend, he's never said a word to me about my eating. My *anorexia*, Dr. Keelor would correct me.

I'm surprised, but I guess I should be relieved. I *am* relieved. Drew hasn't asked any tough questions and I'm hired.

I'm hired. I look up and down the aisle and tut. Somebody's left a messy rectangle of dirt picked out of hooves, and shavings brushed from a tail, right in the middle of the otherwise clean floor. I pick up the broom propped just outside the office door. I'll fix that.

I work here.

Journal – Wednesday, July 3

▷ 22.1 lbs down from initial weight.

▷ 8K run, 60 sit-ups. Cycled to barn and back—G-mapped it: 8K.

▷ Thank God I got the job. Now I'll be out of the house every day. No
   Annabelle watching everything I eat.

Food highlight: No lunch—by the time I got back from talking to
   Drew, Annabelle had taken Jamie out.

Food lowlight: Pasta for dinner. Hard to resist Annabelle's spaghetti
   sauce. Ate more than I should have.

Calorie intake: Trying not to think about it.

chapter

five

The furniture in Dr. Keelor's office is covered with tightly stretched leather in a smooth grey color. The exposed arms and legs of her chair, and the sofa Annabelle and I sit on, are shiny chrome. The dark floor clicks under Dr. Keelor's high heels, and is completely silent under the Birkenstocks Annabelle and I wear. When I slip my foot out of my sandals and give the surface a tentative touch with my bare toes, it's cold and smooth. I lay my whole foot on it, spread the ball of my foot wide, as Drew is trying to teach me to do inside my paddock boots when I ride. I lift my foot away and it leaves behind a small oval-shaped spot of moisture, which rapidly wicks away and disappears, leaving the slick tile unmarred: perfect.

The doctor is talk, talk, talking. Showing Annabelle a study about anorexia and OCD. "Some experts feel one is a manifestation of the other, while others believe they're comorbid illnesses," she's saying. Uh-huh. Sure.

Annabelle looks interested and, come to think of it, she probably is.

I, on the other hand, am fascinated by the pattern of the rain sliding down the big slanted windows. They stretch from the ceiling right to ground level, which, on this floor of the hospital, is at about waist height. The office is gorgeous in a sterile, semi-subterranean, ultra-modern way. It could be in a James Bond movie as the lair of the nefarious villain. It suits Dr. Keelor. I wonder if her house looks like this.

Dr. Keelor looks at her clock. It took me about four visits to realize it even *was* a clock. It's made of two white and aluminum concentric circles, with the inner one telling the hours, the outer one the minutes. It's bizarre, and I can't actually tell time on it, except that when she looks at it, I know we have about five minutes left in our session.

I love Dr. Keelor when she looks at her clock.

Now she'll sum up. We'll stand up—any exposed skin making a small tearing sound as it pulls away from the sofa's slick leather. Annabelle will say a sincere thank you and I'll mutter, "Yeah, thanks." *If lightning struck those who fibbed, I'd be full of holes.*

I lean forward to catch this week's summary—I've learned I can spend fifty-five minutes contemplating the wrist angle Drew wants me to achieve, outlining a history essay in my head, and planning how I'm going to manage not to eat dinner tonight—if I just listen to Dr. Keelor's last five minutes. It gives me something to discuss with Annabelle on the drive home, and satisfies her that I'm participating in my therapy.

"Have you considered supplementing?"

What?!? I hold it in, but just barely. The effort sends a twitch through me, and Annabelle notices.

She looks sideways at me before saying, "Pardon me?"

"Putting supplements in Grace's food. That could help." Dr. Keelor sits calmly with her pen poised over her clipboard. I wonder if she has an order form for the supplements in front of her. Wonder if she's waiting for us to tell her if we want one box or two.

I'm sitting right here. I can hear you. I want to say, just in case the doctor's made a mistake by letting slip the supplement idea in front of me. *I'm the one trying to starve myself—remember?*

"Well, I guess if Grace was interested in having supplements in her food, she would put them there herself." Annabelle answers slowly, enunciating each word carefully, like she's also not sure whether the question was supposed to be asked in front of me, and whether she should answer.

"Interesting," says Dr. Keelor and makes a note before saying, "Well, I'll see you next week."

♦ ♦ ♦

We peel out of the parking lot, and I slot Annabelle's

change away in her purse. Six dollars from a twenty-dollar bill. If I stopped seeing Dr. Keelor, we could take Jamie to Disney World.

I usually try not to emphasize how much I dislike Dr. Keelor. Seeing her reassures Annabelle. Besides, I've heard that expression, "Better the devil you know." I see the doctor as a well-groomed, cold-hearted devil, but I could be wrong; there might be someone much worse in the next office down the hall. Still, after that session, I can't resist. "OK, you have to admit, that was pretty weird."

Annabelle glides to a stop at the parking lot exit. Signals a right-hand turn. Flexes her fingers, then curls them back around the steering wheel. The corner of her mouth turns up. "Yes. It was. Incredibly weird." She pulls out and merges into traffic. Her nostrils are flaring now, and her smile's so wide, it reveals her white teeth right back to her canine. "If you notice some powder on your pasta tonight, it's nothing—just this really fine Parmesan I bought."

I snort and the Diet Coke I've been sipping nearly sprays out my nostrils. For a few seconds, we're both speechless, laughing as we drive through the city traffic, and, at times like this, I think, *We're OK. Everything's fine. I can just stop worrying.* I almost feel like I can stop fighting my ever-present hunger pangs. Want to tell Annabelle to pull over, right there at that Subway, and go in and get me a foot-long BLT.

Almost.

On second thought, maybe not today. But soon. There's a

twelve-inch sub in my future; it just has to be when I decide
the time is right.

Journal - Thursday, July 4

▷ 22.3 lbs down from initial weight.

▷ 8K run, 60 sit-ups.

▷ Hunger pangs manageable with water.

Food highlight: skipped breakfast completely by stretching shower
out until it was time to leave.

Food lowlight: had to eat lunch and dinner—home with Annabelle
watching me. Can't wait to start work!

Calorie intake: approx. 1400 :(

chapter

six

You wanted this.

Yes, I did.

I wanted this, and it's the best job in the world. The sun is shining and the sky is blue. I'm surrounded by fit, gleaming-coated show horses, grazing behind neat, white wooden-railed fences. I'm being paid to ride, and this is just the first day of many … but Bella is *slow*.

Frustratingly, maddeningly, turtle slow. Not slow because she can't go any faster—she's sixteen-two, with lovely long legs—but slow because, at twenty-five, she figures she's worked hard enough in her mature life and has become astute at doing the bare minimum to get by.

Crunch … crunch … crunch … crunch … There's no spring

to those steps. She's merely putting one foot in front of the other because I'm carrying a crop and am not afraid to use it if she stops dead in her tracks.

Her plodding walk is all that's needed to stretch out her tendons, though, so at least I'm doing my job. And the leisurely pace gives me plenty of time to observe Sprite being lunged in the sand ring.

I've rarely seen so many people surrounding one horse. Sure, maybe on those shots CBC does from behind the clock tower at Spruce Meadows. When they're filming the CN International with a million dollars in prize money. Maybe then, there will be several bodies thronging around one horse.

But this is a small show barn in Eastern Ontario. Sprite may be a horse I love, but he's a horse like a thousand others in this province. He has the potential to win some championships and, possibly, go on to compete at the Royal in Toronto. That's if he has a good year *and* he doesn't get injured *and* his new rider can control him. That hardly warrants four—or is it five?—onlookers; a couple holding clipboards, one with a camera, and several wearing breeches and gleaming knee-high boots.

Bella pauses as we pass a particularly lush stand of grass—testing me. "No, you don't ..." I pull her head up and away from the tempting blades and glance back at Sprite, just in time to see him pin his ears back and kick at somebody who's edged too close along the fence line.

Which one is his new rider? I reach up to shade my eyes

against the morning sun, when Andy's voice snaps me back to the job at hand. "How's it going?"

"Fine." I straighten my shoulders. *Don't slouch. Never underestimate any horse.* Slow as she is, Bella has been assigned to me to walk because the novice adult rider who originally volunteered to exercise her didn't work out. Bella exploited his inexperience by simply refusing to move any further than the first patch of lawn. When he got annoyed and used his crop on her, Bella heaved him off with one huge buck, and continued grazing until she found a clump of clover.

A bit of that energy would be welcome now, but it's nowhere in sight.

"When you're done with her, why don't I introduce you to Iowa?" Andy says. "It'll be good for you to see what tack I use on her."

As far as energy goes, Iowa should be more like it. She's Andy's "project" for this year; a horse Andy buys cheap, then trains, shows, and re-sells for a nice profit. In order for Andy to get bargains on her project horses, they pretty much have to be young and / or inexperienced, and usually both. While there's every chance she'll settle down later on, Iowa is still a green five-year-old and, as such, holds more challenge. I urge Bella to get a move on and finish her last trip along the driveway.

But when I get in and untack Bella, the wheelbarrow's standing at the end of the aisle. Every other stall has been mucked out except the last one. Andy's nowhere in sight and Iowa's dozing, one hip cocked, lip drooping over her empty grain bucket, so I finish off the last stall.

It doesn't take long—it's not that dirty—just a bit of selective scooping and pitching, and a bag of fresh shavings fluffed and banked, and it's ready for its occupant to return from turn-out. I dump the dirty bedding in the manure pile and leave the wheelbarrow neatly propped against the wall where it belongs.

Then I find Andy. She's in the indoor arena, lunging a mare that came in a couple of days ago on trial. When she sees me, her face lifts. "Oh, great, Grace. Can you grab my saddle from the office and hop up on her? I don't like the way she's going, and I'd like to see her under saddle."

And this is the way the day continues. While there may have been defined reasons Drew and Andy wanted me here—e.g., Bella, Iowa, Sprite—clearly, what they really need is just an extra body. A body who knows how to look after horses and ride them, and who can jump into whatever's needed at a moment's notice. A couple of times, I open my mouth to say, "But I'm supposed to be ..." and then stop because what I'm supposed to be doing is whatever they need me to, and that's exactly what I am doing.

It's hectic and, at the end of the day, I'm left with the feeling of having accomplished very little, while never having stopped for a single minute.

I know what Annabelle will say. Something like, "Wow! Are you ever going to learn a lot!" And she's right. Also, at this rate, I'll probably be too exhausted to want to show on the weekends. I'll be glad I don't have to. And there's the carrot of Sprite, dangling out there in front of me. He won't have an entourage showing up every day to lunge him. Sooner or later, I'll get to ride him again.

I swing up onto my bike, grateful the way home's downhill, as I wouldn't have enough energy left to get there otherwise. Behind me, someone yells, "Hey!" I turn around, thinking, *Who, me?*

And, yes, he means me. A tall figure wearing worn jeans and a white T-shirt stands in the doorway of the barn. The legendary Matt Ancott. He tilts up a wheelbarrow and yells, "Thanks!"

I barely remember mucking out that one stall several hours ago. "Anytime!" I call back.

I hope I've made a good impression on my first day. It's made an impression on me in the form of a thick layer of sweat and grime, muscles that will be aching by tomorrow, and a general feeling of exhaustion.

Journal - Friday, July 5

▷ Too tired to write. Must have burned a gajillion calories today …

chapter

seven

My first ride on Iowa. From the perfectly circular
dapples on her grey rump, to the natural arch
of her neck, to the long black lashes rimming
her inky eyes, she's one hundred percent cute. Not my
type of horse—I like them bigger, tougher; I like feeling the
power coiled up inside them. Still, the potential in Iowa
is undeniable. She's pretty and she moves like a dream; I
could sip a cup of tea while sitting her trot and not spill a
drop. She's unbelievably calm for a green horse.

Andy hasn't given me any instructions for riding her,
other than, "Just get to know her a bit." So that's exactly
what I'm doing. In the most literal sense of the expression,
I'm taking her through her paces.

Walk: lively and willing. Ears pitched forward, a slight spring in her step, back hooves tracking up nicely into the prints left by her front ones.

Trot: nice transition. Straight into it with no hesitation. Very, very smooth. Still energetic, without a hint of pulling.

Canter: picks up the right lead first try—a nice feature in a five-year-old. Has a classic "rocking chair" action: forward and back, forward and back. Nothing to complain about there.

Is she perfect? No, certainly not. She needs a lot of guidance with her steering; holding her in a straight line over trot poles is a feat. And she's noticeably stiffer on her left lead than her right. But many horses with much more experience have these shortcomings. In fact, most will retire without ever having grown out of them. In other words, she's pretty darn good.

"What's wrong with her?" I ask Andy, who has come over and is leaning on the fence. I shrug my shoulders and smile as I ask it, so she'll know what I really mean is, "There's not much wrong with her."

Her face lights up. "I knew you'd like her; she's good, isn't she?"

Before I can respond, we're distracted by hooves scrunching gravel. Someone calls out, "Door!" and Sprite is ridden into the ring. He's also being led. This is unusual. All but the most rank of beginners ride their own horses to and from the ring. It's also a mistake. Sprite's clearly riled up already by the double fuss of someone on his back and someone at his head, and is taking little mincing sideways steps with his hind legs, rotating around his front end, and making circular tracks in the deep sand.

Andy steps back from the fence, and I give Iowa a cluck and a squeeze, and we move into her lovely, eager, forward walk.

I can't ignore Sprite. And, because I'm distracted, Iowa is, too. Her ears flick constantly from the path ahead of her to him, to me.

My fixation is driven partly by my itch to get a good look at the girl riding him and see how he goes for her (*please don't click with her like you do with me*) and partly by my need to protect Iowa. I've never been in a ring with Sprite without being the one on his back. It's unsettling to be in striking range of his quick teeth and lightning-fast hooves.

More importantly than finishing the summer with added experience and a spate of ribbons, Iowa must come through sound and unscathed, so I give Sprite a wide berth.

The man who led him in—a resemblance between him and the rider suggests they're father and daughter—has stepped to the side and is talking to Andy, as Sprite and his rider proceed around the track.

The girl is tense; not just in her lips and face, but through her arms, back, and seat, too. Sprite's jigging along in a half-walk, half-trot that's both uncomfortable to sit and unsettling to try to control. He's already lathering up where the reins rub against his sweaty neck. *Relax. If you relax, he will, too.* Easy to say; hard to do.

Part of me doesn't want him to relax. Sprite is mesmer-
izing in his misbehavior. I love the flash in his eyes, the way
his mane won't lie flat, and the exaggerated flex of his neck
muscles as he over bends—dropping behind the bit in an
evasion it's tempting to let him get away with because he
looks so darn flashy when he does it.

Sprite's rider keeps him in the gate end of the ring, so
I take Iowa up to the far end and practice a long series of
twisty maneuvers—circles, serpentines, figure eights—to
supple her on both sides and help her fine-tune her balance.

We're getting into it; she's moving nicely and starting
to give on her tough left side, and I'm focused in on the
regular rhythmic rise and fall of her gait, concentrating
hard on balancing my hand, leg, and seat pressure to keep
her consistently moving forward without getting runny or
strung out.

And that's when Sprite explodes into my line of view.
He's flat-out belting. His veins bulge. His ears are pinned.
We're directly in his path. Is Iowa trained to back up? I
don't know.

I use all my aids at once and will her to move. She
doesn't. *Come on. Don't wiggle in the saddle. Don't confuse
her.* Try again, clucking this time. From this angle, Sprite
looks like a snake, head thrust out at the end of his long,
straining neck. Iowa takes one hesitant step back—*good
girl*—then picks up steam, nearly tripping backwards as she
tucks her haunches underneath her and reverses.

Sprite zips past us, right for the back fence. Straight.

Unwavering. Not giving an inch. Playing chicken with the boards.

Will he go over? Will he turn? Will he go through? *Don't think about that one.*

Over or turn? Over or turn? I suck in my breath, tense every muscle as I wait to find out.

Sprite doesn't give a hint away before he needs to.

With literally inches to spare, he veers. His turn is quick. Agile. Right-angled. The girl on his back hurtles forward as Sprite dekes out from under her. Her body hits the wood with a splintering crack.

For suspended seconds that tick by like minutes, nothing happens. Everything's quiet. The silence lasts as long as it takes the thrown girl to find her breath. Then she starts gulping the way you do when you're simultaneously crying and gasping for air.

Andy and the man spring into action. On her way past me, Andy says, "Deal with Sprite."

I shake my head. Of course. Help. I scramble to dismount. The jar of my awkward landing shoots through my heels, knees, hips, and back, settling somewhere in my back molars. *Ooof!*

It's surprisingly easy to catch Sprite. Now that he's dumped his rider, his plans for fun have been foiled by finding the gate firmly shut. He stands with his head poking over it and, when I lead Iowa up beside him, lets me grab hold of his looping reins with no fuss.

He's so docile, I have no problem opening the gate and

leading both horses through and up the hill to the barn, Iowa on one side, Sprite on the other.

I glance back to see Sprite's rider walking across the ring under her own steam. That's good. Andy, who renews her first-aid certificate yearly, would never let her try that if there was any chance of serious injury.

I'm glad she's not hurt, but I wonder how she must feel to own a horse she can't even ride in a quiet school at home?

For the first time since finding out Sprite was sold, I'm sorrier for his new owner than I am for myself.

Journal – Monday, July 8

▷ 22.8 lbs down.

▷ 8K run, cycle to work and back (8K).

▷ No time to be hungry!

Food highlight: No lunch—no time at work, anyway.

Food lowlight: Not choosing one; it was a good day!

Calorie intake: approx. 1200.

chapter

eight

I wake up to the car door shutting, front door opening, and muted shufflings in the house. Annabelle's home. I babysat Jamie this evening while Annabelle went to book club. Andy hosted tonight—at lunch, she carried a plate of double-chocolate cookies out to the barn. "There are only four of us coming tonight, and I baked three dozen cookies. Help yourselves."

Karen emerged from the stall she was cleaning to grab a couple.

"Mmm, yes, please," Drew said, stuffing two in his mouth, then declaring through crumbs: "She makes the best cookies in the world; it's why I married her." High praise indeed from Drew.

"Grace?" Andy held the plate toward me.

"I'm good, thanks."

"Such willpower," Andy said.

"Oh, I just had a huge lunch today." I rubbed my T-shirt. "I can't fit anything else in."

It was, of course, a massive lie. My stomach was pinched with hunger. But it was hard to say what felt better: the compliment from Andy or the lovely hollowness of my insides. I went back to my sweeping, humming with satisfaction.

Now footsteps come up the stairs and along the hall, and the water runs in fits and starts before the house falls quiet again. Almost quiet, that is. There's a tiny rhythmic pinging from my ceiling fan as the chain hits its casing once on each rotation. Despite the fan, I'm hot, and a skunk has been by; its pungent odor settles in my nostrils, tickling them and keeping me awake.

I'm hungry.

This is the problem with being awake. Sleeping keeps me from thinking about food but now, when I'm not sleeping, my stomach is insistent. It growls and gurgles. A girl in school used to laugh at the noises her rumbling belly made every morning in home room and say: "My stomach is digesting itself!" That's how mine feels right now.

I slide one foot out of bed. Then the other. I'll have a glass of water, then check on Jamie while it settles. It might mean I have to get up to pee later on but, if I'm lucky, it'll trick my stomach into submission for long enough to let me fall asleep.

Jamie's peaceful. His skin is sticky with a dew of perspiration on it, and he's snoring, but these traits, so unappealing in grown-ups, are unaccountably sweet in a three-year-old. As usual, his head is shoved into the corner where his bed meets the wall, and all his important friends surround him. Sniffles, Bear, Puppy, and Sheepie, and, lurking under the covers, denting my palm when I bend over to kiss him, are what he calls his "bumpy" dinosaurs. Terence and Matilda, brother and sister Tyrannosaurs, and a variety of other meat-eaters, since they're his favorite. Plant-eaters have to watch from the sidelines, where he's arranged them carefully in family groupings on his bookshelf and toy chest.

As I ease his door shut behind me, my insides give a deep wrench. I'm still hungry; there's no denying it tonight. So, what next? The kitchen. Was there any doubt I'd end up here?

This afternoon, Annabelle made a huge salad to take to Andy's. It was just the kind of salad I adore, and also the kind I've been avoiding eating for some time. Full of high-calorie things like avocados and cheese, with a tangy dressing. I helped her—peeling, pitting, and slicing the avocados—and all the while, I imagined how they'd taste with that dressing on them. How smooth they'd be in my mouth.

When she was done tossing it all up together in our biggest stainless steel salad bowl, she lifted down one of the pretty ceramic ones she uses for company and transferred the salad in. It didn't quite fit so she put the rest into a smaller bowl and stuck it in the fridge. "You can have this for dinner, if you like," she said.

Of course I hadn't because then my resolve was firm. No way was I eating avocados and full-fat cheese. Not a chance. For dinner, I had some lettuce, cucumbers, and tomatoes tossed up with plain balsamic vinegar, and a bowl of unbuttered popcorn while watching the movie. Even when Jamie didn't finish all his Kraft Dinner (who doesn't love KD?) I resisted spooning up the leftovers.

I loved myself then. Even though there's always a lump here or an inch there to work on, at times like that, I can at least bask in my strength and control.

Now, though, everything's different. I swing open the refrigerator door and am mesmerized by the bright light inside. Everything around me—the familiar surroundings of the kitchen, the moonlit shapes of the yard and woods outside—retreats into darkness. I lean against the door and stare at the salad, still sitting in the bowl. Jamie's KD is there, too, just crying out for some ketchup.

I'm shaking. I reach my hand out and pull it back. Do it again. I'm so hungry. I don't know if I can do this anymore. At this moment, the decision I'm facing—to eat or not to eat these several hundred calories—looms as large any I've made in my life.

What will happen if I do? I'll have to run an extra 5K tomorrow or risk gaining half a pound—maybe even a whole one. Worst of all, if I eat this salad, I will have given in.

And if I don't eat it? Once the answer would have been simple. Triumph, victory, willpower in the face of temptation. If it was still that straightforward, though, I would have shut the door long ago. Would never have been down here, barefoot in the middle of the night, to begin with. Because the faintest little voice in my head is whispering that this control isn't mine—it's not something I can take credit for. The control comes from something inside me that shouldn't be there and, maybe, just maybe, defying it would be the victory.

I don't know how long I've been sitting in the moonlight on the window seat in our kitchen when Annabelle walks in. She seems half-surprised to see me, but is also obviously half-not. "I had a feeling someone was up."

I turn and she says "Oh, Gracie, why are you crying?"

"I'm all mixed up."

"I know. Do you want to talk?"

I shake my head and tears spill into the grooves alongside my nose.

"Why don't you go back to bed, then?" she asks. "Everything always seems worse in the middle of the night."

"I can't." My stomach takes over, almost louder than my voice, growling through the quiet kitchen.

"Oh," she says. "Hungry?"

"Yup." I hesitate, then add, "I've been staring at your salad, not knowing what to do."

"I see." She bustles around the kitchen, making soft thumps and scrapings. I stare out the window, seeing nothing, past the point of my former angst, now just feeling nothing, too.

I hear her come near, place something on the table. I turn to look at it. Compromise on a plate. A sliced apple. A rice cake. A mug of steaming skim milk. I can eat this. I sink my teeth into the apple, taste the tart juice. My stomach turns over in gratitude.

"Thanks," I say.

"Anytime." And she sits with me and says nothing as I finish every bite.

Journal - Wednesday, July 10

▷ 22.8 lbs down (holding pattern—sigh …).

▷ 5K run (cut short so I could babysit Jamie), cycle to work and back (8K).

▷ I was HUNGRY all day. Difficult (severe understatement).

Food highlight: No lunch again—never eat lunch at work.

Food lowlight: None. Midnight snack.

Calorie intake: approx. 1100, 1300 after snack.

chapter

nine

Sunday morning, while everybody else is at Cedar Mills on a glorious sunny-but-not-too-hot July day, winning ribbons and racking up championship points, I ride my bike over to the barn to exercise Sprite.

While she didn't suffer any serious injury from being catapulted into the fence, Sprite's owner is badly bruised and sore. So I've been tasked with schooling Sprite while she accompanies the rest of the barn to the show as a spectator.

My bitterness about getting him ready for her to show is still in place but it's fading, and a tiny part of me is relieved that at least nobody else is going to win any red ribbons on him today.

I always keep up a low-key conversation with my horses while I groom but, today, feeling free in the unaccustomed quiet of the barn, I speak up. Chatter to Sprite about the weather and the burrs wound through his tail. "Where did you find all these?" Sing-song, "You're a real pain in the butt, aren't you?" as he tries to nip my bottom while I pick out his front hoof.

At the gate of the sand ring, I almost turn back. It's been dragged and the sand sweeps in perfect corduroy furrows down the long sides and around the corners. I don't think I've ever been the first one to mark up a ring before, and I've definitely never done it solo.

I pat Sprite high on the neck. "I guess we might as well enjoy it." I cluck him forward beside me to the dead center of the flawless ring.

He goes sweetly, almost angelically. No antics, no fussing, not a foot out of place. We would have won every class we entered. And, of course, there isn't one single, solitary soul to even acknowledge our smooth performance.

I'm just finishing up, sweeping the dirt from the aisle and singing the Beatles' "Blackbird." It rings loud and happy—and off-key, too—in the empty barn, but who cares? I love the uplift and hope of this song. It's been Annabelle's bedtime lullaby for as long as I can remember; she sang it first to me and now to Jamie each and every bedtime, and I still love hearing her version—as off-key as mine—drifting down the hall at night.

"Take these broken wings and learn to fly ..." Sprite's ears pitch forward. He likes the song, too.

"You have a way with him."

I spin around. Oh, God, *that's* what Sprite was looking at. Or rather, *who*. Matt Ancott. My personal riding hero. Drooled over by at least half the girls at the barn. Beloved by their mothers. Perfect, but not so perfect he's boring. *That* perfect.

Crap. Was I really singing? Out loud? Double crap.

I shift the focus to Sprite; hope Matt won't notice the red flaring through my cheeks. "He's a fantastic horse."

"You're right," Matt says. "He is. But not everyone can handle him, and most people don't bother trying."

"Well, I enjoy it. I enjoy him."

"That's the main thing. Just keep thinking that way and you'll do fine."

And then he turns and he's whistling as, broom in hand, he leaves to go sweep up elsewhere.

And it's only after he's left, when I gather my thoughts again, that I recognize the tune floating behind him:

"Blackbird singing in the dead of night ..."

Journal – Sunday, July 14

▷ 23.1 lbs down (a whole new pound conquered ...).

▷ 10K run, 8K work bicycle.

▷ Not STOMACH hungry but wicked cravings all day.

Food highlight: Still no lunch ...

Food lowlight: Giuseppe's Pizza for dinner. My undoing. Can. Not.

Resist. Giuseppe's. Ate one and a half slices. Feel sick. Can't count today's calories. Say bye-bye to 23 lbs down … it was fun while it lasted.

Calorie intake: If I write it down, it'll be TRUE. Can't go there.

They limp and stumble down the ramp off the trailer as a small Monday-morning group of concerned onlookers stands in the stable courtyard. Their stringy legs hardly support them. All the parts of a horse that should never droop do: ears, tails, lower lips. They tremble all over. They've been unloaded in the sand ring to prevent them from escaping but, turns out, there's no need to worry about that. This lot's going nowhere.

I'm not sure where they came from, exactly, or why they're here. I wouldn't be here myself if it weren't for my run-in with Matt yesterday. Just as I was getting ready to go home, swinging my leg over my bike and starting the flurry of pedaling needed to gain momentum on the deep gravel of the laneway, he stepped out of the barn door, still with broom in hand.

"You might want to make sure you're here nice and early tomorrow morning. Someone like you might find it interesting."

He'd disappeared back into the barn before I could get out any of the dozens of questions his speech left me with. Not the least of which was: what exactly are the qualities of "someone like me?"

So, of course, I got up early, skipped showering and breakfast, and jumped straight on my bike to come here. Who could resist such an enticing invitation? I stand a couple of steps back from the fence; Matt gave me a brief nod when he walked by on his way into the ring, but I'm not entirely sure if I'm meant to be here.

I twirl a length of my hair around and around my finger. In an effort to stop that, I circle the ring finger and thumb of my left hand around my right wrist. It's something I do just to check they still touch, with room to spare. Next I try to reach my thumb to my pinkie finger. Surely that's tighter than it was yesterday? I can't remember. My breathing quickens.

My mounting panic's broken by the arrival of Mr. King, the rarely seen owner of the barn. He uses a cane to walk up to the fence; his nose is large and lumpy; he wears thick glasses and has white, wispy hair. I have to admit, up until now, I've never paid that much attention to him.

But today, he's a presence. He stands up straight with

anger. He's gentle only to the dirt-encrusted animals straggling in the yard; nobody else gets too close.

I'm standing next to Drew—not *right* next to Drew, as I'm getting more and more interested in the proceedings and really don't want to be shooed away now—but close enough that when Mr. King walks over and starts talking to him, I don't have to strain to hear their conversation.

"I would never have sold them if I'd imagined this," the old man says. "They were beauties, every one of them, when they left this place, and that woman—a vet's wife, no less—said they were just what she needed to start her riding school." Mr. King nearly spits on the words "vet's wife." Like him, I can't imagine someone whose household is, or should be, devoted to doing good to animals, allowing any horse to get into the state of these six.

"How did you find out?" Drew asks.

"Just by chance. My granddaughter's friend was moving to Thunder Bay, wanting to ride there. I said she should look up this riding school where my horses had gone. Her mother called me a week after she got there, said it was one of the worst things she had ever seen. I told her, 'Pay what you need; I'll cover it. Buy them back and ship them to me,' and, bless her, she sorted everything out."

"So they're not old?"

"Not half as old as they look," says Mr. King. "You wait and see; you get any of them into shape to use in your lessons and you'll be amazed what they can do."

Drew nods and Mr. King moves off, heading back toward

the sorry group of horses. On his way, he calls out to nobody in particular: "This is the start of their new life; they'll all have new names!"

He walks up to each one, lays a hand on six thin necks, barks out names. "Hope," "Glory," "Joy," "Jubilee," "Triumph." At the sixth, he hesitates. I wonder, has he run out of names? She's a little mare—what's left of the shape of her hindquarters speaks to quarter horse breeding. She raises a well-boned head, all dark eyes and, outlined through the dirt, a broad blaze. Her ears swivel, nostrils flare—once, twice—then she whinnies so boldly, the power of her breath raises the white waves of the old man's hair.

Mr. King takes a step back and laughs. He laughs so forcefully, it's more like a snort—if he were my teacher at the front of the classroom, I would giggle, but here it's a movingly powerful thing to hear. "Whinny!" he yells. "This one's called Whinny!"

Then he turns to face Karen and Matt. "Now, clean them up and bed them down. And feed them, for God's sake, but not too much or they might colic."

There's so much work to be done. Six new horses on top of the thirty-nine others that still require feeding, turn-out, bandaging, lunging, and more. And Matt's meant to be out with the tractor replacing fence posts. I'm so glad to be here. To be needed. Very pleased I turned down Serendipity to take this job instead. Happy I was here schooling Sprite yesterday, instead of at the show with everyone else, because otherwise where would I be right now? Definitely not doing anything this interesting.

A bank of normally unoccupied stalls in the back barn has been opened up for these six and, after a transfer done in slow, limping stages, they stand in a long row. These are old standing stalls, rarely used because boarders prefer boxes, and most of the school horses live outside all summer. Still, they're deeply bedded and wider than most standing stalls, so there's plenty of room for the horses to lie down. Most horses won't—lie down, that is—in new surroundings. It's a little bit of their wild heritage they hold with them. A survival instinct still not bred out of them. However, one, Hope, is already down; whether she's lowered herself or collapsed is hard to say.

"You OK for us to go?" Matt asks once all the tail guards are snapped closed, and I nod yes.

He hands me a pile of halters before he and Karen head back to their regular tasks, and I move in and out of the stalls, talking to each animal, stroking their sides as I come through. I bring a soft brush with me and clear the crusted mud from their faces before I fit a halter to each. I look for the oldest, most broken-in halters, so the fabric will be as soft as possible against their thin skin.

Hope doesn't even bother to struggle to her feet; just lies quietly and, once I have her halter fitted, rests her pretty palomino head in my arms, her big brown eyes trained on me, and heaves a deep sigh.

"Good girl. You're such a good girl. We'll take care of you

now." I tickle the underside of her jawbone as I talk, and she closes her eyes and sighs again.

I swallow hard. It really doesn't take much to make them happy.

Once I have them all clipped in to the front of their stalls, with ropes long enough to let them lie down, but not long enough to trip on, I trail the hose down the aisle and trickle fresh, cool water into their buckets.

Now what? I'd like to feed them all until they burst, repair all the damage done over weeks and months with high-speed, high-calorie feeding. It wouldn't work, though. They need to come back slowly, carefully. There's no quick and easy fix to the condition they're in.

All could use a good grooming, but most look too miserable to be touched. Whinny, however, is definitely perkier than the others, and her tail, almost solid with burrs, begs to be combed out. The flies will eat her alive with nothing to swish at them.

It's going to be a long job, so I pull up a hay bale and place it at the back of the stall to the left of Whinny's hind legs. Then I sit down cross-legged and begin the meticulous process of disentangling her tail, one long hair at a time.

In the rush to look after the new horses, I forgot to refill my water bottle. My stomach grinds with emptiness. I shift on the bale; the hay prickling my skin, the persistent itch on my nose, and the lone determined fly that dives in every time I pick up a handful of tail, make it impossible to sit still.

Weepiness creeps up on me. These poor horses. They didn't ask for this. I picture them standing in a wind-whipped winter field with not a shelter or a scrap of hay in sight.

When Matt comes in from the fields, the pile of broken hair and burrs on the floor beside me is almost as thick as the tail Whinny has left. I start to say something, but my breath catches and tears sting my eyes.

"I know," he says. "I know."

Then he holds out his hand. "Come on, now. You've done a good job. She'll be much more comfortable."

I let him help me up since my shaky legs fell asleep long ago. The debris of twigs, leaves, and horsehair showers from my lap. I bend over to give my still-shaky legs a big brush and, when I stand, force a smile. "Thanks," I say. "I feel better now, too."

Journal - Monday, July 15

▷ 22.9 lbs down (couldn't hold on to 23 lbs, as predicted …).

▷ 6ᴋ run (home late after extra work with Whinny), 8ᴋ on bicycle.

▷ No calorie discussion out of respect for the starvelings. Their ribs. The sink in their haunches. They're not me and I'm not them, but it's a bit too close to the bone .

chapter

eleven

Whinny's a small liver chestnut with a white blazed, slightly dishy face that hints at Arab breeding somewhere in her background. A sideways look at her suggests she's going to fill out to quarter horse proportions. In other words, a million miles from the scopey bay thoroughbreds I dream of.

But I like her. Something clicked when I first saw her. Now, as soon as I'm done riding my regulars— Bella, Iowa, and, ever since he threw his rider, Sprite— and schooling, hand-walking, lunging, and grooming whichever horses Drew and Andy have on my list, I seek her out. I groom her, feed her carrots, and take her out on a lead shank to tear at the lush grass growing around the stone foundation of the old barn.

On Friday, I'm just knocking the dirt out of my brushes, preparing to leave, when Matt appears. He visits Hope as often as I come see Whinny, so we cross paths frequently these days.

"Thought I might find you here," he says.

I laugh. "Just finishing up."

"That's what I figured. I'm almost done, too. I came to offer you a drive home."

"Oh, I'm fine. I've got my bike."

"I know you've got your bike, but I'd still like to drive you home."

This is directness I'm unused to. Saying no would be awkward, and I can't think of any particular reason to do so. "Oh, well, then, sure."

"Give me twenty minutes?" When I nod, he picks up his pitchfork, heads back to the main barn.

"Thanks!" I yell belatedly to his retreating back.

I grab the watering can and swing it side to side, spattering a delicate pattern on the dirt-layered concrete floor. Then, satisfied the dust will stay down, I grab the broom. One fast pass up the side, swishing the debris toward the stalls, and then I come at it from the other end, sweeping bits of hay, dust, and shavings into the end of each of the standing stalls; erasing the day's mess in a few quick minutes.

"Nice work." How does Matt always sneak up on me like that? And why do my cheeks always flush red hot when he does? "Ready to go?"

"Yeah, sure, just wait one minute," I hold up a carrot in explanation, sidle up alongside Whinny, and let her chomp a huge bite. I drop the rest in her feed bucket and turn to face Matt. A wave of butterflies rushes through my stomach. *Don't be stupid.* It's just Matt and he's just being nice. He's a nice guy; it's one of the reasons I like him.

Out in the yard, Matt waves at the truck. "Hop in. I'm just going to double-check the latch on the shed. It's been sticking."

I climb up into the huge Spartan cab. It contains no gadgets, just a steering wheel and a gear stick. I turn around and see my bike lying in the back of the truck. *When did Matt put it there? Why does he want to drive me home?*

My left fingers fly to encircle my right wrist, seeking the reassuring sharpness of my wrist bones poking just under the skin. Their hardness brings to mind the knobs of Whinny's hipbones, jutting from her haunches the way no horse's hipbones ever should.

I shiver, drop my hands into my lap, then tuck them under my thighs.

Matt's door creaks as he yanks it open. "You OK?"

"Fine. Just … just thought I forgot my chaps." Nudge my toe at a heap on the floor. "But I didn't."

"Do you mind if we don't go straight home?" Matt's already indicating to turn right, away from my house, instead of left, toward it.

"Uh, no, that's fine." *Why? Where are we going? Who cares …?*

I've looked up to Matt for so long. Over the past several days, I've also come to like Matt as a person, not just as some abstract riding hero. I trust Matt. And, I have to admit, sitting here next to him in his battered jeans and his faded T-shirt, I think Matt is drop-dead gorgeous.

You and every other girl who's ever met him. I know, I know. It's not hard to think of about a million reasons Matt would never like me. Or at least ten:

First five—Matt:

▷ Amazing dark eyes

▷ Just the right amount of freckles

▷ Rides like a god

▷ Is nice, smart, funny, and everybody likes him

▷ Not interested in me, anyway.

Second five—me:

▷ Way too many freckles

▷ Much room for improvement with regard to riding

▷ Am rarely funny and, when I am, usually end up insulting someone by mistake

▷ Am either too fat (my opinion) or too skinny (opinion of assorted adults)—either way, body clearly leaves much to be desired

▷ Not interested in him, anyway. Really. *Not.*

So, considering all the above, I'm pretty curious when he pulls off the bumpy dirt road we're traveling on to turn onto another, even bumpier and much narrower lane that dwindles to nothing by a huge tree growing beside an old fence.

He turns off the engine.

Quiet. Quiet. The quiet's unbelievable. For about fifteen seconds, anyway, and then the first tentative birdsong creeps back in. A cricket starts humming. The landscape, and the wild things that inhabit it, shift back into business, absorbing Matt and me and his pickup truck into the movements and noises of the summer afternoon.

"There's something I want to show you," Matt says.

"OK."

"This way." He hops out of the cab. We're stopped on a slight angle, so I'm pushing uphill as I creak the heavy passenger door away from me. The drop to the ground is higher than I expected and a nettle stings my skin on the way down.

"You OK?" he asks.

"Uh-huh." Stacking hay in the loft, helping repair jumps and, of course, crawling around on my hands and knees with Jamie, ensure my legs are always a mess of scratches, bumps, and bruises. The nettle sting just adds to the overall effect.

When I reach his side, Matt is balanced on the top rail of an old wooden fence. "It's out there," he says. What I see is a hay field, not yet cut, neck deep in places, and swaying in the breeze.

Of course it's beautiful, in the way everything unspoiled in the country is beautiful, but it appears to be a hayfield like many others I've seen—very much like the ones surrounding both my house and the barn. It's with an equal mixture of interest and uncertainty that I follow Matt up over the fence and jump, feet first, into the depth of the grasses.

I was wrong. I was so, so wrong. There's nothing ordinary about this field. I can't believe how long I've lived alongside fields like this one without ever stepping into one before.

Pushing through the rustling grasses is like swimming in greenery. I lean forward into the wind, barely feeling my feet and legs supporting me, using my arms to part the way and propel me forward.

The field around me is dizzying, like the disorientation I've felt in the ocean when waves dance and ripple all around, and the sand beneath my feet shifts under my eyes. My progress through the field, half-surfing, half-wading, with the grasses brushing my bare skin, has made my whole face smile. When Matt turns to me, the same smile is on his lips, pushing up through his cheeks and into his eyes.

He motions to me to stop and rests his hands on my shoulders and turns me, ever so slowly, in a complete circle. We're in the center of the field, on what must be a slight rise, because all around us, that moving, living, dancing carpet spirals out and out until, on all four sides, it hits trees. Not a road or a fence or a building of any sort—not even the truck—is visible from here.

I think of all those times I've heard of places referred to as "the center of the universe." For me, this might just be it.

Matt leans in closely, cupping his hand around my ear to

be heard over the wind-driven rush of the grasses and the exclamations of birdsong. "Amazing, isn't it?"

"Amazing!"

I'm not sure if he can hear me but he clearly understands. He gives me a thumbs-up and a pleased smile, and something inside me breaks away and dissolves. A piece of armor I had no idea I possessed is gone, melted in an instant by one simple instance of delight.

I look at Matt in a whole new way now. Smart, still, yes. Talented, of course. Good-looking, especially here in the sun and the wind. But a gift-giver, too, kind and generous.

"Thanks!" I yell and the wind whips my word away and scatters it across the field.

♦ ♦ ♦

Matt pulls into our driveway to a scene of happy chaos. The sprinkler is going on our lawn, with several small boys belting through it, wearing only their Spiderman underwear. Two large dogs run in circles just outside the spray zone, barking their heads off.

The smell of barbecue hangs in the air, and on the far side of the sprinkler is a gathering of adults, Annabelle in the center of them, laughing and balancing a tray of drinks as she serves her guests.

"Oh, God," I say. "All my crazy neighbors." I wait for Matt to take the out. To say, "I'll leave you to it," haul my bike out of his truck and accelerate out of here.

Instead, he sniffs the air. "Smells good."

"If you're hungry, they'll feed you. They love barbecuing." I tuck my crossed fingers into the hollow between the small of my back and the seat of the truck.

"Sold!"

Wow! Straighten my fingers, open the door. *He's staying.*

When we reach the edge of the patio, I declare, "Matt, these are our neighbors. Neighbors, meet Matt."

There's a chorus of "Matt!," "Hi Matt!" and a general rush to rearrange chairs, make space for us.

Before we can even sit down, Annabelle presents Matt with a plate overflowing with a hamburger and a hot dog; "Go ahead; have both. We cooked way too many."

The smell of charcoal and sizzling meat wakes my dormant stomach. When Annabelle produces a bowl of perfectly sautéed mushrooms, I nearly cave. My mouth waters. They'll taste so good. But I don't need them. I'm strong enough to resist. Nothing ever tastes as good as you think it's going to, anyway. Looking and smelling are fat-free so I look and smell all I like, and grab a heap of salad—no dressing—before anyone can comment on my empty plate.

I grab Matt a Coke, with a Diet Coke for me, and we've just settled into lawn chairs, when Jamie launches himself, skin slick and cold from the icy well-water coming through the sprinkler, into my lap.

"Hey Gwacie!" he yells. And then, pointing at Matt, "Who's dat?"

"That's Matt," I say. "Matt, this is my brother Jamie."

"Hey, Matt," Jamie jumps up to run back to the sprinkler, leaving me with a large bum-shaped wet spot in my lap.

I keep waiting for Matt to say he has to go, but he doesn't. He eats both the hamburger and hot dog and stays for a bowl of ice cream. He earns what I'm sure will be Jamie's eternal worship by serving himself up as "it" in a game of tag with the bevy of small boys, weaving in and out of the sprinkler and getting his work clothes sopping wet in the process.

As the neighbors collect up their kids and dogs, coolers and lawn chairs, I head to Matt's truck with him. "I'll get my bike out of the back," I tell him.

The afternoon and evening have been great. Unscripted, yes. Uncontrolled, sure. But still easy. Except, now, I'm up against a moment that threatens to undo all that. My bike is unloaded, Matt is poised to step into the truck, and what on earth am I supposed to say?

"Thanks," I say, and at exactly the same time, Matt says it, too.

"I had fun." Again, we both say it at the same time. And then laugh.

"I hope we can hang out again." This time it's only Matt. He leans forward and kisses me on the cheek. I'm left breathless as he swings up into the big pickup and backs it, bouncing and creaking, out of our gravel laneway.

I wave and wave and am still waving when Glenda, the neighbor down the road to our right, comes up beside me.

"Nice one, Grace," she says, and I pretend I don't know what she means but, really, I think it's the perfect summing up of a perfect day: "Nice one."

Journal - Friday, July 19

▷ 23.2 lbs down. Took all week, but I've clawed my way back.

▷ 8k run, 8k work bicycle.

▷ Found a stick of gum left in the pocket of my breeches. A bit sticky (yuck!) but I forgot how well it pushes back the hunger.

Food highlight: Resisting sautéed mushrooms!

Food lowlight: Finishing the half of Glenda's brownie Jamie left on his plate. Tried to tell myself it was OK—not my brownie—but the calories (about 175) are the same. Stupid me.

Calorie intake: 1100 + 175 craving calories = totally preventable.

chapter

twelve

When I go to Whinny's stall on Monday, it's empty. Panic rises in me. The other five who arrived with her are here; there's no way she's fit enough to go out with the herd of school horses; she can't be ridden. Where is she?

I hear Matt whistling his way down the aisle.

"Matt!" I remind myself: *don't run in the barn, don't shout in the barn*; instead, do a very fast half-shuffle and call his name in an exclamatory whisper. "Matt!"

He turns his face to me and I wonder, did he always have those three freckles right across the bridge of his nose? Is that dimple in his chin new? "Hey, Grace. Just the girl I was looking for."

My breath catches. "I was looking for you, too. Do you know where Whinny is? She's not in her stall."

True, his expression is serious, but he was *whistling* just now. Surely "Blackbird" wouldn't be running through his head if Whinny had been cast in her stall and broken her leg trying to kick her way out. Or if she'd colicked overnight and hadn't pulled through.

"Come with me," Matt says and I follow him, gripping my right wrist with my left hand again. *Quit doing that.*

He leads me out of the barn and around the corner to a little-used back paddock.

"Whinny!" The little mare stops pacing the fence line and swivels her head to me. With her foreleg raised and her nostrils flared, she's wildly beautiful. "Look at her," I breathe.

"I think she likes you, too," Matt says. "That's the first time she's stopped since they put her out."

I look more closely; her coat is dark with sweat. There's foam between her hind legs.

"What happened? Did something scare her?"

He shakes his head. "She just started weaving and pacing as soon as Karen left. Whinnied non-stop for a while, but she's mostly stopped that now."

Even as he says it, she pauses, lifts her head, and bellows a ringing call across the stable yard. Her body shakes with the effort of it, and the shrill cry sends a corresponding tremble through me. From deep in the barn, muffled by walls and distance, a whinny sounds back. Hope? I'm not sure. Definitely one of the other starvelings.

I look at Matt. "Aaaah. She's lonely." Whinny's a herd animal and, right now, she's separated from her herd.

He nods. "Seems that way."

"So let's get her in. She doesn't have the strength for this. She's going to kill herself."

"Believe me, I know. Andy knows, Drew knows, Karen knows. Problem is, she won't let any of us catch her. Every time we try, she gets more worked up. Andy decided it was best to leave her for now. Kelly's coming later, so if she thinks it's serious, she might have to tranq her."

"But ..." I start, then stop. If they all tried and couldn't do it, what do I expect? Still, it seems wrong to leave her like this. She starts moving again, in a steady pace, up and down the fence, spinning when she reaches the end to start back again.

"But what?" Matt asks.

I shrug, sigh. Frustration floods me and I stamp my foot. "I don't know. Nothing, I guess." I sweep my arm out toward the hepped-up mare. "I just ..."

"If you're willing to try something, I'll help you."

"Yes! Anything!" I turn to face him, grab his arm, jump up and down in front of him. "What is it?"

He takes a step back, holds up his free hand. "Whoa! Take it easy. This is going to take a while. How's your patience?"

"Fine!" I snap.

He arches his eyebrows and I take an exaggeratedly deep breath. "It's good. I'm patient. For things that are worth it."

"OK, then. Wait here." He retreats into the barn and returns with a lunge whip.

"What's that for?"

"You ever heard of joining up?"

"Of course."

"You ever seen one done?"

Will he let me do this if I haven't? There's only one way to find out. "Does TV count?"

He laughs. "Let me guess: *Heartland*."

Crap. Yes. "No!" I protest. "I saw *Wild Horse Redemption*, too." Does watching tough tattooed prisoners in Colorado use join-ups to tame wild mustangs buy me more street cred than *Heartland*?

It seems to. "I think you should try with Whinny," Matt says. "I think she's ready."

Whoa, I think. In principle, I think it's a great idea. I'd love to try it. But me? Me being responsible for a join-up with this sensitive and starved little mare?

"I don't know ..."

"I'll help you." He waits. When I don't say anything, adds, "I'll be right here."

Comfort seeps into me at his words. I take an involuntary step toward him.

"You're going to do it," he says.

I reach out for the whip. "I'm going to try."

The last thing he says to me before I duck between the fence rails is, "It'll probably take longer than on TV."

♦ ♦ ♦

He's not joking.

An hour passes in fits and starts of high energy, nervous walking from Whinny. Most join-ups I've seen are done at the trot, but the corduroy of her ribs and the caved-in hollow behind them make me limit Whinny's effort as much as possible.

With her head held high on her skinny neck and her stiff gait, she has a giraffe-like air. Every time she completes five circuits, give or take, I ask her to change direction. I take a step toward her—blocking her forward progress, symbolically rather than physically.

At first, this sends her into a mincing trot, accompanied by a lot of head tossing and tail swishing. Over time, she settles into the routine, though. Now I just have to give her a look and lean in her direction, and she obligingly changes direction to pace the opposite way.

She still has dark sweat streaks on her neck, but she's much calmer than she was when I first got here. I, on the other hand, am getting hotter and hotter. The sun's rising— beating down on the middle of the paddock where I'm standing—and even though I'm not walking the fence line like Whinny, I haven't stood still once during the entire process.

Matt comes by every now and then. "You hungry?"

Yes! "No, I'm fine."

"Thirsty?"

"It would be great if you could refill my water."

The water sits where he left it, though, balanced on a fence post near the gate. I want it but I don't want to break the communication I've established with Whinny.

I get her to change direction one more time and, as she heads back to the fence line, my vision blurs. The sun's ticked up one more notch and, when I reach back to gather my hair up, it's hot to the touch. I spread my feet to improve my balance and concentrate on the fresh air cooling the back of my neck. When I shake my head, my eyes clear.

"You OK?" Matt, checking in again. He looks at me for a long minute. Please say he didn't see me sway just now.

"Yup. Just hot."

"You haven't eaten all morning."

I pull my eyes from his. Refocus on Whinny. "Nope."

"You haven't touched your water."

"I know. I meant to, but the time was never right."

Whinny hesitates and I call, "Hyah, girl!" and wiggle the whip through the sand behind her.

"She doing that a lot?" Matt points at the mare and tugs his ear to indicate her inner ear, cocked toward me.

"Most of the time now."

"You're doing great," he says. "She wants to trust you. She can't do it on her own, though. She's looking for you to give her a way out. Don't give up; she needs to see you'll stick around long enough to make it work."

"Oh, I'm not going anywhere."

"Me neither. I think it's time."

Matt's words send a jitter through my guts. I exhale forcefully in an attempt to settle my nerves. I've been here for coming up to an hour and a half. I want this to happen. But what if I drop the whip and turn my back and nothing happens? What if she just goes back to pacing the fence?

What if she rejects me?

"I'm scared." It's not the kind of thing I'd normally tell anyone, let alone someone I'd like to impress. It's embarrassing and wimpy.

"It's OK," Matt says. "It'll be fine. I'm right here. Just do it."

I take a deep breath and open my fingers. Let the whip drop away. Take a deliberate step away from Whinny, leaving my hand open behind me.

Try to read Matt's expression. *Is she coming? Is it working?*

All I see is calm reassurance. *It's OK*, he mouths.

Then I hear it. *Squeak, grind, squeak.* Hooves crunching through sand.

I hold my breath.

Breathe, Matt mouths. Takes an exaggerated breath, leading by example by filling his own lungs.

I smile and breathe and a bristle of whiskers brushes my palm. The tingle runs up my arm and shivers through my shoulders. Then, the velvet softness of Whinny's muzzle pushes right into the cup of my hand and she exhales a deep sigh through my fingers.

Oh, my God! The joy rises up through me and stalls my breathing again. Oh, oh, oh!

"Good girl," I say.

"Now, walk away," Matt's voice is calm, low.

I can't. She's here. She's come this far. How can I walk away? I hold Matt's gaze and put one foot in front of the other. Start walking.

She comes with me as though it's the most natural thing in the world. Her head bobs by my side.

"Stop." Matt instructs and I stop, and Whinny stops beside me, ears pricked forward with an inquisitive look on her face, as if to say, "Where next?"

I'm giddy with relief and success and exaltation. I walk, stop, walk, stop. Run to the end of the ring and she trots beside me. Turn to head back and Andy's standing beside Matt.

Stop once on my way back to the gate so Andy can see Whinny halt square and patient beside me, then keep walking, up to the gate and through it and on into the barn with Whinny at my side.

I take her straight into her stall and pat her and fuss over her. "You've earned a bran mash."

When I step back out, Andy's standing there. "Is that OK?" I ask. "Can I make her a mash?"

"You can. And something else." There's a seriousness in her voice that stops me short. Have I overstepped my bounds? Should I have been mucking out stalls this morning instead of playing join-up with Whinny?

"You've earned a project. She's yours to work with, if you're interested. Ask for help if you need it; do what you think is right, and see if you can get her ready to be used in lessons by the end of the summer."

"Wow! I mean, yes. Great. Thanks."

And head off to the feed room to assemble a bran mash for my new project.

Journal - Monday, July 22

▷ 23.9 lbs down. So close to 24.

▷ 8ᴋ run, 8ᴋ cycle, an hour running around with Whinny in the paddock.

▷ I think my breeches were looser today. Think. I could be wrong.

Food highlight: Feeding Whinny up—bran mash.

Food lowlight: Dinner not great. Why does Annabelle have to serve perogies? Talk about carbs …

Calorie intake: 1200—blame the perogies.

chapter

thirteen

At the beginning of my next meeting with Dr. Keelor, she looks at me gravely and crosses her hands over her belly (which has several months' worth of baby growing in it) and asks: "Does it bother you that I'm pregnant?"

A giggle rises in me—the first time I've ever experienced mirth in Dr. Keelor's office—and I swallow hard to smother it. I cross and uncross my legs to buy time, then clear my throat. Can I answer without laughing?

"No." So far, so good. My voice is calm. "I know the difference between being fat and being pregnant."

Dr. Keelor nods solemnly and makes a note on her clipboard. Annabelle's finger taps mine, but there's no way

I can look at her without laughing out loud. I focus instead on the dandelions proliferating outside the big windows; try to count the brilliant pops of yellow.

Questions like the one she just asked show why nothing useful is going to come of my seeing Dr. Keelor. *Does it bother you that I'm pregnant? Do you want to put supplements in your food? How would you feel if you gained five pounds?*

No. No. And *fat.* Questions answered. Leaving long, boring segments of our hour-long sessions to be filled in with my own thoughts.

I need to work on my leg position with Iowa. It's just slightly off and, when I concentrate and tweak it, she relaxes all over and drops right into her frame.

What's that? Am I ever hungry?

Real answer: *Yes. Starving.*

Answer for Dr. Keelor: "Not really."

Whinny's going to be gorgeous when she fills out. I love her proportions and, even as skinny as she is, she's got a nice deep chest and good head carriage. We'll need to work on developing her neck muscles.

Whoops, almost missed that: What do I see when I look in the mirror?

Real answer: *Somebody shorter than Annabelle, heavier than Mavis. Somebody who doesn't look good in anything she wears. Somebody no one would want to take care of.*

Answer for Dr. Keelor: "I don't know." Shrug. "Just me, I guess."

Matt. Matt braiding flowers into Hope's tail. Matt letting me drive his truck on the dirt lane leading to the field of swaying grasses. Matt giving me a leg up, and me remembering exactly where he placed each finger two hours later, long after my ride was over ...

Why is Annabelle staring at me?

"... better for Grace to stop horseback riding."

What?

The doctor consults her clipboard, flips back and forth between pages as she adds, "Grace has continued to lose weight. She's dropped below eighty-five percent of her ideal weight. It's not appropriate for her to continue activities that strain her body."

I sit forward, grip my knees. "I'm not ... I don't! It's not like that!"

She doesn't *shush* me exactly; she just holds up her hand. "As you know, I will be on holidays for the next few weeks." Dr. Keelor skipping right over me to address Annabelle. "While I'm gone, I recommend a close monitoring of Grace's eating and weight, and I'd like you to consider seriously what I have said about her riding. We can discuss this during our next meeting in August."

Does that mean I have until August to figure things out? I have no idea. Annabelle's lips are tight, eyes down, as she rifles in her bag, searching for the check she hands over at the end of each session.

As Dr. Keelor makes yet another note, the effort required to keep from jumping up and ripping her clipboard from her hands is ten times more strenuous than any "activities" I ever do at the barn.

♦ ♦ ♦

"You're not going to, are you?" I can't bring myself to actually say the words "make me quit riding"—that would make it too real. Besides, I don't need to; Annabelle knows exactly what I mean.

Annabelle changes lanes, notches the radio volume down two levels. "I don't want to."

"She doesn't get it."

"No, Grace, you're right. I don't think she does. But ..."

"But what?"

"But she's right about one thing. A body needs fuel to work."

I open my mouth to protest, but she holds up her hand. "Would you ride Whinny or Hope in a lesson right now? Would you jump them?"

"Oh, come on, Annabelle! That's totally different. They *need* me to take care of them."

I pause to let her answer. She changes lanes again. In silence.

"They need to be protected."

Pause again. Annabelle checks all her mirrors, then stares straight ahead.

"I can look after myself."

Annabelle makes a funny choking noise but says nothing. I open my mouth for one more try, then shut it again. My entire future rests in Annabelle's hands. It's time to shut up and hope.

In lieu of talking, I fidget. I stew. I stare into my lap and shudder at the spread of my thighs pushed against the upholstery of the passenger seat. I circle my fingers around my wrist and am certain the fit is tighter than yesterday.

As we pull into the driveway, I know the way to earn brownie points—to reassure Annabelle that everything's fine—is to stay at home and eat a healthy lunch, but I just can't.

Fear and turmoil and anxiety and the need to move, move, move, and keep burning calories, send me catapulting out of the car and onto my bike.

"I'm going to the barn!" I yell, and lose myself in the turning of the pedals, the wind in my face.

I ride to the barn on autopilot. When I arrive, I have no recollection of crossing the highway, with its whipping cars, and even the hill I normally curse all the way up is completely absent from my memory. I've ridden so fast, I have a good hour before Drew and Andy will expect me to start work.

I go straight to Whinny.

She looks terrible. She's been lying in her shavings, which are none too clean, and has manure stains covering the entire left-hand side of her body. She smells, and so does the stall, so I put her on cross-ties and muck out her stall, then take her outside for a good soapy scrubbing.

The soles of my boots are full of horse manure, my legs are

splashed with dirty water, and my T-shirt has a suspicious smear down the front. "How could I give all this up?" I ask Whinny. "Huh? There's no way, is there, girl?"

She noses at me—looking for carrots, but I pretend it's out of affection—and leaves a slobbery streak down my arm. I lead her to the grass and let her tug me along at the end of the lead shank, as she meanders around the yard in pursuit of ever-sweeter patches.

She shifts, heading for some clover, and the sun catches her left haunch. I squint hard, trying to figure out if there's any trace left of the manure stain and, for the second time today, I'm caught distracted and not paying attention.

Two hands close over my eyes.

"Guess who?"

I don't need to guess. The bottom drops out of my stomach. All I want to do is turn around and take a step forward into him.

We're not there, though. As much as I like Matt, we're just friends. *For now...* says the optimistic voice in my head. So, instead of hugging him, I give my head a shake, turn to face him with a smile, and get on with the afternoon. I can use Matt and horses—the sight, smell, touch, and feel of them—to push my troubles out of my mind.

Unless I lose my access to them. *Don't think about it.*

"What's up?" I ask.

"I have to check fences. Want to help?"

"ATV or horseback?"

"Horseback, of course."

"Deal."

♦ ♦ ♦

For a day that started so badly, it improves quickly.

Maybe I should just live at the barn. Everything's normal here. I'm appreciated. I'm needed. When I help Matt muck out stalls, he says, "That goes twice as fast with you around—thanks."

When I ride Iowa, Andy stops by the ring, leans on the fence. "She looks great. How would you feel about showing her one day?"

Ecstatic, excited, over the moon, delirious ... "Great. That would be really good."

When one of the boarders drops off a plate of cupcakes left over from a work function, nobody stops to stare and see if I'll take one. Karen pushes the plate my way and, when I say "No thanks," she just shrugs. "Suit yourself; more for me."

After work, Matt drives me home. There's no kiss goodbye but there is a moment of awkwardness; I'm almost positive it was there. I'm choosing to believe it was, and I'm choosing to take it as a good sign. He wants to kiss me; he's just not ready yet. That's OK with me. I can be patient. Matt's worth waiting for.

As I wave until the tailgate of Matt's truck dips out of my line of vision, and wheel my bike to the garage, I can almost pretend Dr. Keelor's threats never happened. This morning and our appointment in the city seem like part of another time, another world. I hope if I'm really easy to live with, Annabelle will forget them, too.

So, as Annabelle likes me to, I unlace my paddock boots and line them up carefully under the bench in the mud room. I place my helmet neatly on the overhead shelf and resolve to make life easier for Annabelle in any way I can.

I'll clean my room. Although it's not usually that messy. But Jamie's is. So I'll clean Jamie's room. And I'll play with him more so Annabelle can get more work done. I'll mow the lawn before I start work tomorrow. I'll stop dumping my clothes in the laundry inside out. I won't borrow Annabelle's favorite T-shirts and wear them to the barn so they're dusty and smelly when she goes looking for them.

I glide into the house, soundless in my sock feet, thinking of more ways I can help out. There's a pile of my still-unsorted school papers on the hallway table; I'll take care of those.

"I know it's late for you, Doug, but I'm returning your call." Annabelle's voice drifts out of the room that used to be my dad's study. The room where he spent pretty much all his time for the last year or so he lived here. Annabelle's being on the phone with my dad can't be good news.

I freeze, just inches from the study doorway. Moonwalk backwards, still silent in my riding socks, to a spot where I can hear, but not be seen.

Where's Jamie? I crane my head back to peer into the

kitchen / family room and, down at the far end, catch sight
of the back of his head and, beyond it, the Wiggles filling
the TV screen. Annabelle rarely resorts to TV as a babysitter.
This must be a serious phone call.

"Yes, I'm well aware it's 10:30 there, but it is about your
daughter, so I didn't think it would be a big problem."

There is Manchester. Where my dad has a teaching
contract at the university. His excuse for leaving the three
of us here while he—accompanied by a certain young and
pretty grad student (his "research assistant")—returned to
his country of birth to take up the opportunity to teach in
the university's Physics department. "I can't turn it down,"
he said. "Two of their faculty were just awarded the Nobel
Prize."

My overriding emotion when he left was relief. The house
had become dreary and dark with him in it. Nobody was good
enough. If three-year-old innocent, sweet, and adorable
Jamie was "too loud," "too messy," and "disrespectful,"
and if essentially perfect Annabelle was "disorganized,"
"absentminded," and bothered him by spending too much
time volunteering in Jamie's playgroup—"You need to say
'no' more often!"—then how could I stand a chance?

I didn't. If I had even one pimple, I was "spotty." When
I brought home an eighty-seven percent, I was reminded
I'd never get into an Ivy League school—or even a decent
Canadian one—with those marks. Several times, he
suggested I skip dessert: "Girls your age just balloon up
at a moment's notice." And riding ... well, riding was the

"wrong" sport. I should play tennis or golf or take up sailing. "Where is horseback riding ever going to get you?"

The funny thing is, I never once turned down dessert when my dad suggested it. In fact, I often asked for seconds. But the minute he left, I started cutting back. Dessert had been the first and easiest target but, before long, the success I saw from that led me to eliminate snacks and then cut down my meal portions.

These days, my thoughts of my dad are about how much better we're all doing without him. *All we needed was for you to leave.*

"I'm not sure why she called you." Annabelle's voice brings me back to the conversation.

I wish I could hear my dad's answer. I'd love to pick up one of the other phones in the house, but dread being caught.

"Of course you're her father, but you're not here. You're not involved in the situation."

Is the annoyance in Annabelle's normally polite voice as clear to my dad as it is to me?

"Well, I don't know what Dr. Keelor told you, but I can't back her up on this."

I clap my hand over my heart, which is racing double time. Does Annabelle mean what I think she means?

"Listen, Doug, you haven't seen Grace at the barn, and Dr. Keelor hasn't seen Grace at the barn. This job is good for her. She's accomplishing so much. I'm proud of her. I'm not going to take that away from her. Not right now, anyway."

Annabelle's answer is almost perfect. If I ignore the "not right now" part, it *is* perfect. I push my palms against the tears pricking my eyes.

The silence stretches longer and longer. *What* is *my dad saying?* The Wiggles sing "Hot Potato" in the background. It takes discipline not to tap my toes to the annoying, catchy tune.

Annabelle's voice goes icy cold, much scarier than if she yelled. "I don't think you mean that. I don't think it would be good for Grace, and I don't think it's what you truly want."

He must be trying to interrupt her because she pauses, but just for a minute, then continues. "I *am* her mother. You know I am. I've been her mother since the day Olivia died when Grace was six months old."

I suck in my breath.

"Don't threaten me, Doug. If you think you could do a better job ..."

I inch closer to the door.

"Gwacie!"

I take two quiet giant steps back from the door. "Hey, bud! How are you? I just got home from work!"

Will Annabelle buy it? I have no idea. In the den, she's saying, "I've got to go, Doug. We'll talk more later."

My mind races the rest of the evening. It doesn't still when I'm in the shower. *What was he saying? Is he going to try to take me away from Annabelle?*

For the first time in months, food isn't my primary focus

when we sit down to dinner. I'm so distracted, I bypass my usual five pieces of penne and only stop myself when I've eaten at least ten. *Crap.*

I excuse myself to the bathroom, hover over the toilet with my fingers poised in front of my open mouth, but can't do it. Puking is for cheaters. It's for weaklings. I'll do 100 sit-ups in my room tonight instead and eat less tomorrow.

Normally, I'm asleep the minute my head hits the pillow, but tonight I lie awake for ages, watching the shadows shift across my ceiling, plumping and re-plumping my pillow, and recapping the day:

(1) Was threatened with losing riding. Terrible.

(2) Annabelle said riding is safe. Great.

(3) Dad threatened to take me away from Annabelle? From here? Might lose riding and home? Catastrophic.

No wonder I can't sleep.

Journal - Thursday, July 25

▷ 24.1 lbs down. Another whole pound! Don't tell Dr. Keelor …

▷ 8k run, 8k cycle.

▷ Saw Mavis arriving at the barn as I was leaving. God, she's thin. I'm not going to get THAT skinny. Just five more pounds …

Food highlight: Avoided eating lunch by taking off to work.

Food lowlight: Dr. Keelor looked at my food diary—said she was surprised I was eating apple-cinnamon pitas for breakfast since they have 190 calories each—that's like two slices of regular bread. How did I not know that? Also, why did she tell me? She's so strange … On the plus side: a new, easy way to cut 95 calories out of my breakfast every day.

Calorie intake: 1190—blame the breakfast pita.

chapter

fourteen

While nobody's actually saying it, I don't think Sprite's new owner is ever going to ride him. I school him every weekday now, and once on the weekend—in other words, full-time.

I've learned the girl's name is Rose, and I've also learned she's started riding Serendipity in one of Drew's intermediate lessons. *Serendipity.* The complete opposite of Sprite. Maybe it's wishful thinking, but I can't believe she's going to get back on the horse that hurled her full-tilt into the fence. Not if she likes Serendipity's good manners and mild personality.

As I lead Sprite down to the bottom sand ring on a breezy, blue-skied July morning, I thank goodness—or thank *Annabelle*—that my riding seems to be safe. For now, anyway.

I love this day, this sport; mostly love this quick-thinking, energy-filled horse with his overload of attitude.

The trick is staying one step ahead of him and, sometimes, that's a scramble. Let him take more than four strides in a straight line and he'll accelerate right through my hands and that's it; I'll be riding a riled-up, runaway train of a horse. I've got to constantly bend him, flex him—the right way and the wrong way—weave him through obstacles and make him double back on his own tracks. Confusing him is good. It slows him down while he tries to understand what I want, and gives me a chance to catch my breath and plan my next maneuver. It's golden to find something Sprite's not good at—like turns on the forehand, at which I've discovered he's terrible—because working on them occupies his overactive mind.

We've been at it for a solid twenty minutes, and both of us are getting hot. I think Sprite's compliant enough for me to risk a walk break. I give him a loose rein and am rewarded when he stretches his head and neck right out, low to the ground. It shows he's been working hard. It proves he's relaxing. A good sign.

I relax, too—for about three minutes—then start plotting out my next set of challenges for Sprite. Let's see: we could circle around the blue and white vertical, then double back to squeeze between the red and yellow "x" and the sand ring fence. Then I could ask him to trot over the ground pole laid out for the first jump of the diagonal line. Knowing Sprite, he'll jump the pole. Which wouldn't be all bad ...

... Jump. *Oh, no. No way. I can't.*

I instantly picture the relevant line from the yellowed, fly-specked sheet of stable rules tacked to the main bulletin board—"NO JUMPING outside of a lesson without the express consent of your coach."

But isn't it a bit like that pool rule everyone ignores? "All bathers must shower with soap before entering the pool?"

It's not. I know it isn't. I know riders and horses can be seriously injured, or even die, in jumping accidents. But I want to jump so badly.

And I watched Drew set these jumps up. He used them in his Friday lesson. The distances are perfect for Sprite, and the jumps are tiny compared to what he can do. The footing's in great shape and the gate's closed. *What could happen?*

Strike that. Stupid question.

More like, *who will ever find out?*

Nobody, if we're quick and careful. So we'd better be quick.

Sprite, picking up on my turmoil, pricks his ears forward, lengthening his stride into an energetic, swinging walk. I gather my reins, and he knows it's go time. I won't let him trot, so he jigs sideways. "Settle down," I order, but he just arches his neck higher and grabs at the bit.

I pick my first fence. Just one. That's all. The minute my eyes lock on it, then up and past to find a sightline in the distance, Sprite bounds into his canter. I forgot how quickly he covers ground on his way to a jump. Three, two, one, and—*whoomp!*—I'm launched into the air, with the curve of his body solid under me. Sprite's been denied jumping so long, he's doubled the height he needs to clear this one. I push my hands forward against his neck so I won't catch his mouth on the landing. The leap is so big, my helmet tips forward as we come back to the ground.

I should circle, should settle him back into a polite trot. Should snug my helmet back into place. But we're on a perfect line for the next fence, and he's going beautifully, and I ache to do it again, so I point him at it and say, "Let's go!" and he deer-jumps that one, too.

We clear all ten fences with not just inches but feet to spare. We twist in between and turn, and Sprite makes all his corners; even if some of them are far too fast and involve an excessive degree of lean.

He's happy to be pulled up after finishing the course. He drops obediently to a walk and whiffles breath out through his nostrils—a satisfied, contented sound—and I copy it and giggle. There's nothing like the high of jumping a horse like Sprite.

I throw back my shoulders, survey the landscape, and freeze. *Shit*. Holy crapping shit. Matt's there.

All my earlier rationalization and reasoning flee. I wasn't supposed to be doing that. What is Matt going to say? Oh, God, what if he tells Drew? What if I have to stop riding Sprite?

Might as well find out right away. I ride Sprite through the gate where Matt meets us.

"Hi." My stomach churns. My knees quiver.

"What were you thinking?"

How to answer? "I'm sorry. I couldn't resist. I shouldn't have. I ..."

"No, you shouldn't have. It was so dangerous to jump all by yourself down here. What if you fell? Who would help you?"

"I ..." There's nothing good to say. *I didn't think? I should have known?*

"God, Grace, next to smoking in the barn, this is about the dumbest thing I can think of you doing!"

I inhale sharply, straighten in my saddle. "I would *never* ..."

"What? You'd never do *that* stupid thing but you would do *this* one?"

I've never seen Matt angry before. It shakes me. And I've got no defense. "I was wrong. I won't do it again."

He opens his mouth, then closes it again. Covers his forehead with his hand and squeezes just above his eyes.

Sprite paws the ground and I wait.

Matt's chest rises and falls in a deep breath. He drops his hand away and looks at me. "You scared me. You jump him so fast, so big. It's amazing and it's this close to disaster." He holds up his finger and thumb with no space left between them.

"I know. I get it."

"You can't do that alone."

I nod. "I'm sorry."

"Don't say sorry. Just don't do it again."

"I won't."

Matt steps over to the gate. Pulls it shut and loops the chain through twice.

I open my mouth to ask if he's going to tell Drew and Andy, then change my mind. Instead say, "Are you angry with me?"

He looks straight at me. "I don't have an exact word for what I am with you."

Right at the end—as he says "you"—just before he looks away, I swear, he smiles. Just a bit. Maybe.

As he walks past me to head back up toward the barn, he adds, "By the way, that ring is closed for the day. Just in case you were thinking of jumping the gate."

This time, I'm sure he's smiling.

Journal - Sunday, July 28

▷ 24.5 lbs down. Progress. SLOW progress.

▷ No run but jumped Sprite! 8K cycle.

▷ Feel like I can do anything after jumping Sprite, like lose the last five pounds.

Food highlight: Extreme low calorie day. Feeling light.

Food lowlight: None. Happy. Good. Annabelle and Jamie at Upper Canada Village all day. Didn't have to eat AT ALL.

Calorie intake: 0 (Zero!)—just looked back to a couple of months—1700 calories! Unbelievable …

chapter

fifteen

I'm floating on air. My insides and outsides are light. I'm on a roll; after no food yesterday, I managed to get out of the house this morning without eating, either. "I already ate," I told a still-sleepy Annabelle, and Jamie picked that moment to wake up yelling for her, so I'm still going on zero calories.

As I pump my pedals on the way to work, I struggle to remember the current trendy term for not eating. *Fasting*. No, that's not it. I've read it dozens of times in those horrible celebrity magazines, the ones where they point an arrow to the faintest curve of some waif-like model's abdomen and demand, "Baby Bump?"

As I coast through the front gates, the word swims into my

head. A *cleanse*. Everyone cleanses these days: celebrities, my friends' moms, even our phys ed teacher told us about her cleanse last year. There are sugar cleanses, carbohydrate cleanses, processed food cleanses. I happen to be on an everything cleanse.

Just for now. For a couple of days. Annabelle's declaration that she won't stop me from riding has given me a safety cushion. I ate nothing yesterday and figure I can also get away with it today. Then I can ease back in and maybe eat quite a bit later in the week, and Annabelle will notice and can report how well I've been eating and, maybe, if I can keep that up, I'll be able to stop seeing Dr. Keelor, and then my dad will lose interest and back off.

It might not be a perfect plan, but it's a plan, and the *cleanse* is making me feel lovely and pure and triumphantly in control, and I'm a hundred percent certain my breeches were looser today, so this is the plan I'm sticking with for now. I don't know why I didn't think of it sooner.

I've already ridden Sprite (no jumping) and now I'm at the far end of the upper sand ring, with Whinny pacing circles around me at the end of the lunge line. The gradual work and good food has put a new line of muscle over her shoulder, a gleam in her coat, and a dapple or two on her rump.

"Tuh-rrrot," I tell her with a roll in my "r," and she complies after only the tiniest twitch of my lunge whip. I'm impressed by how readily she's learning—or more accurately, remembering—her commands.

I love watching a spirited horse being lunged. There's a freedom to their movements not often present under saddle, a float to their unburdened strides, and an easy carriage of their neck and tail. Whinny, despite her tough past, has spirit. Right now, she looks free and easy.

The constant circling of a lunging session bothers some people. I've never had a problem with it, but there's a faint buzzing developing in my ears, and a blur of dizziness creeps up on me. I look away from Whinny, fix my sight on a tree in the distance.

Something's still wrong, though. The freshly furrowed ring suddenly seems bumpy, uneven. I take a step backward, seeking sounder footing, and it feels even worse. My ankle twists beneath me, both knees buckle, and I'm sitting in the sand, head down, breathing hard, frightened by the overzealous hammering of my heart.

"Whoa, girl," I manage but have no idea whether Whinny can hear me. My voice sounds far away and echoey.

I'll get up in a minute, I think. Then wait a minute and think it again. I wonder if I'm going to throw up. Wondering what's wrong makes the panic build in me, which makes my light-headedness worse, so I force my breathing to slow. *Don't think about it right now.*

Eventually, Whinny's warm breath blows down my back. She lips at the collar of my shirt before putting her nose down to the sand, whiffing for any bits of hay or grain that might have found their way in and been mixed with the footing.

"Nice girl." Eventually, I might grab her leg, pull myself up. When I'm a little stronger.

"Grace?" The voice is close and familiar. I'm glad to hear it and, at the same time, not. Matt will help, but I don't want him to see me this way.

"Hi," I lift my head and everything spins.

"What happened?" He crouches by my side. "Are you OK? Did you fall? Are you hurt?"

"No," I whisper. Try not to move my head. "Nothing like that. Just dizzy."

And scared. My heart's still pounding far too quickly.

"Hang on." I'm aware of Matt leading Whinny away, then, in a minute or two, he's back without her.

"When was the last time you ate?" he asks.

I shrug. I can't remember. I also can't muster the energy to trot out one of the ready-made lies I've become so good at over the last few months. "I ate at school," "I ate at the barn," "I ate before you got home."

"Recently?"

"Probably not," I say. *No*, I think.

"Here." He puts an orange juice drink box under my face, straw in, ready to go. Even in my weakened state, I recoil. There are over 100 calories in that thing. I can't drink it.

"No, thanks." I keep my head down, fixating on a grain of sand to keep my world from spinning. "I'll be fine."

"Grace," Matt's hand is firm on my chin. It might be nice if I wasn't so woozy. "This is not a joke. It's not a request. It's an order. Take a sip, now."

I obey.

It tastes so good. Cold and pulpy. The one-two punch of the orange's sweetness and sting slides over my taste buds, trickles down my throat.

I mean to take the smallest sip possible but, before I know it, I've taken two and then three.

In a minute, the sugar hits my brain and strength seeps into me. I lift my head, take a deep breath of air, look at Matt.

"Thanks. That's much better. I don't know what hit me."

He's not going to be fobbed off that easily. "Yes, you do, and so do I. You're starving yourself."

It sounds so blunt, so wrong, stated straightforwardly like that with nothing sugar-coating it. Without the label of "disorder" or "illness" or "problem" to soften it.

I shake my head and the dizziness rushes back in.

"You're drinking the rest of this." Matt pushes the orange juice back under my face. "And then you're eating a power bar." He pulls one from his back pocket. "And then we'll talk."

"What if I say no?"

"Then I'm driving you home," he says simply. "And I'm going to talk to your stepmom and Drew and whoever else it takes, and I'm going to tell them it's not safe for you to work around horses when you might pass out any minute."

He can't. But he will. Matt has a look on his face like I've never seen before. He's determined. There's no sway there at all. No uncertainty I can exploit. He's made his decision and he's not going to second-guess it.

I believe Matt. He'll do what he says. He'll take all this away from me. My summer of riding. Whinny and the work I've done with her. Gone. Along with my freedom, because if Matt kicks up the fuss he's threatening, I can guarantee Annabelle will kick my treatment into overdrive. Like me, Annabelle doesn't trust the un-horsey doctor, but Matt's word will be gold.

He's not done, though. There's more.

"I talked to Drew about Sprite." He pauses, looks meaningfully at the juice box. I get it; if I want something, I have to give something. I lock eyes with him and take a sip and, as I swallow, Matt continues. "I told him I thought Sprite should be jumped. Drew says if I'm there to watch, you can do it."

Bingo. Matt's just ratcheted things up a notch and he knows it. He might not know why; probably doesn't get that the only thing that makes me feel lighter, stronger, more adrenaline-filled than losing another pound, is flinging Sprite over a course of jumps, but he's seen me jump. Knows how much I love it.

Matt's handing me exactly what I want on a silver platter, and all I've got to do is eat the Caramel Peanut Fusion power bar he's holding out to me. *Shit.*

I don't want to give it up. The words sear through me, tumbling my emotions, bringing tears dangerously close to the surface. Despite the hunger, despite the worry on Annabelle's face, despite here, now, nearly fainting in the sand ring, my disorder—if that's what I have to call it—has given me so much. Structure, goals, regular small achievements. It's shown those who judge me—Drew, my dad—I can accomplish anything I set my mind to.

But Sprite, Whinny, Iowa. Matt. I can't lose them. Not today. I'm weak and hungry and very confused. I'm not convinced of the right long-term decision. But I do know what I have to do in this moment.

I hold my hand out for the power bar and look Matt straight in the eye. I take a bite and chew.

It's delicious and I hate every mouthful.

Journal - Monday, July 29

▷ Twenty-seven pounds down. It suddenly seems like a lot. What have I done? What am I doing?

chapter

sixteen

The next morning, I work through my usual duties. I walk Bella, adding in the five minutes of trot I'm now allowed to throw in. I work Iowa, with Andy scurrying around, setting trot poles on the straight, on bends, spaced long, spaced short. "We need to get her into a couple of jumping classes before the end of the summer. This will get her ready."

Then I ride three horses for a prospective buyer, hopping up on one, then another, while Andy keeps up a seamless chat with the client. Using my best show skills to work like crazy and make each horse go perfectly, without ever appearing to expend an ounce of effort.

"Do you think they'll buy one?" Matt asks as he comes

into the ring to relieve me of one of the two hopefuls I've been left holding.

I wasn't sure how Matt would act today. Was afraid there'd be awkwardness between us after yesterday's incident, but he seems perfectly fine; I guess everything's back to normal. I'm relieved.

"Quinn went really sweetly."

Matt nods. "He always does."

But we both know Quinn's not likely to be sold today. The other two are taller, prettier, flashier. Also worse-behaved, questionably sound, and one's a cribber. Smart, reliable Quinn would be a better mount for most young riders— would have been a much better fit for the girl who bought Sprite—but this parent, like most others, will probably look right past him, find a vet to declare the big, showy bay sound, and end up paying for extra schooling when her daughter can't control him. If the horse stays here, she may end up paying me to ride him.

The horse Matt's leading stays in the front barn while Quinn lives in the back. "Meet me at the picnic table when you're done," Matt says and, twenty minutes later, I do just that.

"What's this?" I ask as Matt pulls containers, napkins, and a couple of small flasks from a big knapsack.

"Lunch." Before I can shake my head and say, "No," he says, "Yes, Grace. Yes."

He's got that look on his face again—the one from yesterday, and when I see it, I chant to myself: *Sprite,*

Whinny, Iowa, Matt.

I keep my mouth shut.

Matt starts divvying things up. A massive sandwich, bursting with fillings, stays on his side of the table.

I get a thin bagel, raisin and cinnamon flavored, with nothing on it, not even butter.

He has a container of trail mix and a granola bar.

I get an apple.

He tops things off with a ziploc bag, lumpy with chocolate chip cookies.

For me he has a cup of yogurt and a spoon.

"And this," he says, pushing a small thermos my way. There's an ice pack held against it with an elastic band and, when I unscrew the top and look inside, I see milk, its ever-so-faint bluish tinge marking it as skim.

This is OK. I can start with this. I take a sip. It's cold. Delicious. My stomach rumbles in appreciation of my first swallow.

I drink the rest, pausing only to say, "Thanks," partway through.

Matt smiles, "No problem." The milk mustache around his mouth tells me his is chocolate.

In the end, I get through it all the same way: one bite at a time. Once I'm done the milk, the apple seems pretty harmless; I figure it's about ninety-five calories and I can burn those off fairly quickly. I can handle the yogurt as well. The bagel is the hardest. It's so solid.

One look at Matt chewing a bite of his sandwich, which appears to contain cheese, bacon, ham, and avocado, liberally slathered with mayo, and I know he's not going to let me off the hook.

I take a bite of the bagel and it's delicious. Which doesn't help. I've become so used to denying myself foods like this— to suppressing my memories of the tastes and textures they contain—I'm scared this one bite could be the beginning of my undoing.

Not to mention the hunger. It's taken a while, but I've almost come to the point of accepting it; of hunger being my norm, so that being full has become uncomfortable.

If I remind my body what it's like to not be hungry, it's going to be that much harder to go back.

But I know what's at stake, so I bite and chew, bite and chew, and when I'm three-quarters done, Matt says, "That's good enough; let's go jump Sprite."

My mouth drops open. "Are you blackmailing me? Is that what this is?"

He reaches out, covers my hand with his. A shiver runs through me, cut short when he opens his eyes as wide as he can and arches his eyebrows. The smile tugging at the corners of his mouth confirms the fakeness of his sincerity. "Grace, would I do that? I prefer to think of it as *encouraging* you. I'm pretty sure you want to jump Sprite, and I don't see any reason why you shouldn't, so are we going, or what?"

I think of all those times he's succeeded in getting a horse to do his bidding by establishing clear consequences, then offering a way out, usually accompanied by a pat on the neck and a carrot. The same skill I've admired so many times now seems to be at work on me. I'm not sure how I feel about it. I shake my head. "You play dirty."

"I'm wounded, Grace. Really. I just want what's best for you. And for Sprite. It's not that complicated."

Lightning quick, his hand releases mine to scoop up the last bit of my bagel and stuff it in his mouth. I grab for it but am too slow. "Hey! I wanted that!"

"Nice try," he says. "Let's go."

♦ ♦ ♦

"How was work?" Annabelle asks.

"Good, thanks. I jumped Sprite."

"Wow! That's great."

"It was. Matt set up a three-jump bounce combination for him. He hated it at first—barreled through a few times—but by the end, he was paying attention and taking his time.

I scoop up a spoonful of soup, blow to cool it. This is a great dinner for me. Annabelle makes her potato-leek soup low-fat, using buttermilk, and everything else on the table—bread, salad—is help-yourself.

The only downside is the mess Jamie makes with his soup. I inch my chair a little bit farther from him whenever we have this meal. Or spaghetti. Pretty much anything that spatters.

Things fall apart when Annabelle produces dessert. Apple crisp, still hot from the oven. My absolute, hundred percent, no exceptions favorite. Saliva springs to my mouth just looking at it. I know exactly how those lumps of brown sugar baked with butter will crunch, then melt in my mouth. The bubbles of apple filling oozing into the topping will only make it taste better.

But I cannot do this. Not after eating my regular breakfast, lunch with Matt and, just now, a decent helping of soup. I have no wiggle room today. Annabelle knows how much I love this dessert. How am I supposed to just sit while she and Jamie eat it? Anger flares at her for doing this to me.

"Grace?" She indicates the steaming Pyrex dish with her spatula.

I shake my head. I'm afraid I'll cry if I open my mouth even just to say "no."

"You don't want any?"

Shake again.

"But it's your favorite."

"I know it is! And *you* know it is! And I can't eat it, so how do you think that makes me feel?"

She sits back in her chair. "Whoa. Are you trying to tell me I've done something wrong?"

Jamie pipes up, "Me have some."

Annabelle hands him a heel of bread. "Here, munch on this for a minute."

She fixes her gaze back on me. "Listen, Grace. I've tried very hard to understand these restrictions you've placed on yourself. These bizarre rules you live by. But, obviously, I don't." She picks up her fork and grips it until her knuckles turn white. Then, with a sigh, lays it down flat again, lining it up neatly with the edge of the placemat. "Aren't you tired of this? Isn't it exhausting to control yourself at every turn? Don't you just want to be a normal human being and eat a piece of goddamn apple crisp?"

"Of course I do, Annabelle." I push away from the table. "It *is* exhausting." I stand up and turn to walk out of the room.

"So stop it."

"It's not that simple. I'm tired. I'm going to bed."

I'm asleep before Annabelle brings Jamie up for his bath, and I sleep right through the night.

Journal - Tuesday, July 30

▷ I don't think I can do this anymore. Annabelle's right. I'm tired.

▷ Maybe if the numbers stopped? Could I do that? I don't know. I'm not writing any tonight.

chapter

seventeen

As I stumble into the bathroom in the morning, my body feels heavy but not in a bad way, rather in a calm, relaxed, gravity-still-hasn't-released-its-hold-on-me way.

I flush, wash my hands. On autopilot, I prepare for my morning weigh-in. Toe the bathroom scale out from the corner where it lives. Breathe in, then out, whooshing every spare bit of air from my body, willing lightness into my step as I raise my left foot ...

...and freeze. *No more numbers.* The words—or something like them—swim back to me through eleven hours of solid sleep. Leave me balancing, one-footed, as I prepare to get my first number of the day. Success or failure right here in front of me.

I lower my foot back to the floor.

I'm not going to do it. Adrenaline chases away the last remnants of my sleep slowness.

This ends here, now. Movement outside catches my eye. Annabelle walking toward the house. Where has she been this early? *It's garbage day.*

Oh, wow. I've got to move now. Before the garbage truck comes. Before I give in and climb onto the scale after all. Before I lose my nerve.

I dash back to my room—pull on a pair of jersey shorts under my nightshirt—return to the bathroom and, in one quick movement, scoop up the scale and head downstairs.

Quiet. In the kitchen, the kettle's roiling, the morning radio host's giving the weather, and the clinks and dings of dishes and cutlery tell me Annabelle's unloading the dishwasher.

I ease out the rarely used front door. Unlike the side door, which Annabelle refers to as our personal disaster zone, there are no stray shoes here. No handy flip-flops to slip my feet into. It'll be a barefoot trip, then.

Ouch! Yike! Poke! The sharp gravel up close to the house is killer. It gets better further down the drive as two smooth strips emerge, worn flat by the frequent passing of the car tires. I can walk almost normally here. The smooth clay is even mildly soothing to the soles of my feet.

Then I see the snake. I yelp, jump, and drop the scale.

Hesitate to pick it up lest I discover squished snake underneath. Nothing. *Phew.*

The scale is probably broken, though. Or, at least, that's what I tell myself. It makes it much easier to stuff it on top of the bag of kitchen garbage, pushing the lid down firmly on top again so Annabelle won't see what I've done.

I scamper back to the house. The way back is much quicker and easier without toting the awkward scale. I step back in just in time to see Annabelle disappearing up the stairs. Jamie's awake. Perfect timing for me.

By the time she comes back down with my bright-eyed brother chanting, "Cheewios! Cheewios!" I'm in my spot at the table, with a piece of brown toast in front of me, eating an apple one slice at a time. Reading the book I grabbed from Annabelle's library pile in an attempt to distract my brain from the automatic mental calorie-calculating it's become so skilled at.

Are we going to have a fresh start or rehash last night's argument? If it was my dad, I'd pick (b). With Annabelle, I'm betting on (a). I'm right. "I told you if you picked up that book, you wouldn't be able to put it down," Annabelle says.

I smile. Take a bite of toast. "Perfect. That's just what I need right now."

Journal - Wednesday, July 31

▷ No scales, no numbers. So far, so good.

chapter

eighteen

Matt's fallen in love.

Sadly, not with me. It's Hope. He adores her. He's smitten. It's a word I've never used before, but there's a first time for everything, and when a person loves a horse as much as Matt loves Hope, it just seems wrong *not* to use such a perfectly accurate word.

They make a really cute couple. He's so tall and strong with his dark hair and eyes, and those killer eyelashes ... and she's so tiny and blond—she's a true palomino, with a sunny golden coat and creamy pale mane and tail—it's sweet to see him brushing her, being careful not to press too hard on her especially bony bits, and to watch how she turns her head to follow everything he does.

She may still be skinny but, man, is she shiny. He grooms her twice a day—before he starts work and before he leaves—and her tail doesn't have one single, solitary knot in it. It's smoother than any ponytail I ever manage in my own hair.

The other things he does for her, well, there's quite a list, including:

- Cook her warm bran mashes, consisting of wheat bran, molasses, grated carrots, and applesauce, all mixed together with some hot water so that it turns into a big *mash* that looks absolutely terrible, yet smells so appetizing, I sometimes want to grab a spoonful.

- Muck out her stall twice a day and bed her down with half a bag more shavings than she's supposed to get (he's so honest that he has the extra cost taken off his paycheck).

- Paint her hooves with tonic so she looks like a wealthy lady who's just come back from a pedicure.

- And, last but not least, he's started bringing a scythe when we visit our field. A scythe and a big burlap feed sack to fill up with the sweet swaying grass that grows so well there. "This is the good stuff, Grace," he tells me, stuffing the sack full. And Hope agrees because, even when she's off her hay, she'll lip up the freshly-cut field grass Matt brings her.

It's nice to see this level of adoration. Watching them together, I realize this is what riding used to be about but, somewhere along the way, it morphed. When I was eight years old and riding on a lunge line, it was normal to fall in love with the pony you rode. Even if that pony was fat and old and not yours, you loved him because you rode him first.

It's been a long time since I've seen a horse worshipped just because she's there. Just because when she nearly fell off the trailer on that fateful day, she caught Matt's eye. I like Whinny, and I enjoy working with her, but it's nothing like what Matt feels for Hope. For me, Whinny is an interesting challenge. For Matt, Hope is a passion.

And it gives me an opportunity.

Because I like Matt. I really, really like him. And not just in the "he has piercing brown eyes and makes me lose my concentration" way. In the "being a decent human being who always does his best to do what's right" way. When you spend time with somebody like that every single day, it lightens your life. Getting to know Matt has enriched me. That might sound stupid, but it's just the plain truth. I'm better for being his friend, and I want to *be* better to deserve his friendship.

For a while now, I've wanted to show him how I feel. I want to give him a gift, but finding the appropriate gift to give a seventeen-year-old guy is pretty tricky. It can't be too personal, or too mushy. It can't be silly. But it still has to be meaningful. And he has to feel comfortable accepting it.

And that's where Hope enters the picture. In Matt's eyes, Hope deserves only the best, so I can safely do something to spoil Hope and, not only will it be accepted, it will be welcomed.

Which is why I've been driving Annabelle crazy, asking her to take me to the tack shop.

My chance comes when Jamie gets a last-minute invitation to a friend's house for a play date. I'm just leaving for the barn when Annabelle hangs up the phone, starts gathering up the essential paraphernalia required for any outing with Jamie—snack, drink, Sniffles the purple T-Rex—and says over her shoulder, as if it's nothing at all, "If you want to get ready and come with me, we can go to the tack shop after I drop Jamie off. Then I'll drive you to work."

"Really?" I ask. "Really? Really? Really? Really?"

"Yes, but you have to put his sunscreen on."

Even this dreaded chore can't dampen my enthusiasm. It doesn't faze me as Jamie shrieks, "Face! Face!" while I immobilize him in a gentle headlock and smear white goo across his cheeks. All I can think of is the money I've been earning, tucked in a special compartment of my wallet, and all I can feel are the butterflies taking flight in my stomach.

♦ ♦ ♦

Later, when Annabelle drops me off at the barn, Matt's wheeling a barrow full of muck to the manure pile. "Where have you been? I'm bringing the herd in for the vet and I thought you might like to come." I blush and he gives me a funny look. "Are you OK?"

"Fine. I just need to get rid of my bag."

"Bring a bucket of oats back with you," he calls as I run to the barn to stash my backpack and its precious contents carefully out of sight, smiling as I grab a bucket and a scoop of oats.

We try the easy way first. Matt throws the big double barn doors wide open and stands at the top of the rise yelling, "C'mon! C'mo-o-o-o-on!" But the horses aren't stupid. They know it's not feeding time. The grass is lush and the sun's warming the day, and they have no desire to leave off grazing and ascend the big hill to pour into their stalls in the middle of a perfect summer morning.

So, we go out to find them. Which entails walking through a vast and quiet field rippled by the warm breeze, with a rhythmic *shake, shake* coming from the bucket of grain I've handed Matt, swinging with every stride he takes.

At first, nothing; not a horse in sight. We do find a groundhog hole, though. Then another one. Matt makes a face and gestures for me to hand him a couple of the long wooden stakes, painted neon orange at the end, we brought along for just this reason. We hoped we wouldn't have to use them.

He shoves them deep into the holes where they'll serve as markers for Ken Scott, a neighboring farmer who comes out with his gun to rid the fields of groundhogs.

I wince and Matt says, "I know. I don't like it, either."

At the edge of the field, where it blends into trees and, quite quickly, becomes forest, Matt throws his arm in front of me. Stops me in my tracks.

He lifts his arm and points ahead, and I start to see them. Horsey shapes in and around the trees, showing through the last scraps of morning mist lingering amongst the trunks. Horses everywhere; the entire herd, stretching back as far as we can see into the woods.

Many of them are old, some pot-bellied, one or two have swayed backs, and almost all of them carry the scars of living in a herd like this: healed-over teeth and hoof marks from equine disagreements over the years. But seen here, in this magical, misty atmosphere, they look beautiful.

"Wow," I breathe. "I feel so lucky."

Matt nods. "We are lucky."

I grab at that feeling of luck, so I can take it with me for the rest of the day and, for that matter, forever. Because, while I feel this lucky, there's no room for feeling fat, or awkward, or ugly.

Another gift Matt's given me. It's time for me to give him his.

It has to wait, though. Because once the herd's in, it's Matt's job to help the vet worm them. This involves Matt dodging teeth and hooves, keeping big horses still and compliant, while Kelly threads long tubes down their nostrils, going in endlessly, endlessly, until, somehow, she can tell they're in the right spot to send the vile worming fluid coursing down through them.

Matt's so busy, we don't even have time for lunch together. He hands me a package, ordering, "Eat this; I'm trusting you," and I tell myself that's why I'm doing it but, truth is, I'm becoming firmly addicted to those raisin and cinnamon bagels.

Despite the risk of being stomped on and having crushed toes, I'd love to help Matt, but Andy has other plans. "Six horses just came in and we're only keeping two on trial. You're helping me decide which four are going back."

So I spend the afternoon riding thoroughbreds straight off the track, who either want to run like they're still racing, or stand stiffly, not understanding what we want them to do in this foreign place called a sand ring.

"What's better?" I ask Andy, "stupidity or stubbornness?"

"Aaahh. The million-dollar question. And one we have to figure out."

In the end, we choose one runner and one stander, and the others get loaded back into the trailer they arrived in.

And I still haven't given Matt his present.

I head back to the standing stalls, where I know Matt will end up, no matter what. I hum as I twist out a hay wisp and go to work on Whinny's coat. I pretend it's all good; I'm relaxed, not a care in the world, but inside, my stomach's twisting and flipping and my breath's coming shorter and quicker than normal.

When I hear Matt's footsteps in the aisle, I nearly bail. Have to force myself to stay where I am; keep working the gloss into Whinny's rump.

"Hey," Matt says.

"Hey. How was worming?"

"Didn't lose any fingers or toes ..." His voice muffles as he disappears into Hope's stall, then stops altogether.

For a minute, we're both silent, then he says, "Grace?"

"Uh-huh?"

"Come here for a sec."

I take a deep breath and give Whinny a pat, step into Hope's stall.

"Do you know anything about this?" He points to Hope's halter. Brand new, leather, and gleaming. With a special padding on the inside of the straps to protect her thin skin from being rubbed raw and sore. It's an expensive halter, and it looks beautiful on the pretty little mare.

"I thought..." I start, then pause before blundering forward. "I thought she deserved it."

Matt's touching the leather, feeling its softness, and rubbing Hope's cheek beneath it. "Pretty girl." He's looking at me, not Hope. He stretches out his free hand and touches my cheek. I push my face against his hand and the warmth and strength of his fingers. I swallow hard and know he can feel it.

From way down at the front of the barn, Andy's voice calls, "Grace! Grace! Are you in there? Chico just threw his rider. Drew wants you to get on him and teach him a lesson."

"I'd better go. Will you put Whinny away for me?"

"Yes," Matt says. "Of course." He's still holding the cheekpiece of the halter, using his baby finger to give Hope a light scratch. "I love it, Grace," he says, and I hug my arms around myself and smile the whole way to the sand ring, where I climb on the badly behaved thirteen-hand pony and show his rider that he really can clear a two-foot fence; you just have to show him who's boss.

Journal - Thursday, August 1

▷ NO NUMBERS. I know what they are—sort of—in my head, but they're not going here.

chapter
nineteen

I catch Annabelle the next morning as she heads out the door, clutching a list in one hand, a squirming Jamie's collar in the other.

"Are you going grocery shopping?" I ask.

"Uh-huh," she nods, then, as Jamie breaks away from her, "Stop it buddy. I promise we'll go to the park when we're done." She turns back to me, rolling her eyes in apology, and asks, "Why?"

I try hard to be casual, like it's nothing, like this is a completely normal thing for me to ask. "Um, I was just wondering if you could pick up a pack of these bagels Matt's mom buys. They're the thin kind, raisin and cinnamon," I pause. "Only if you see them, though. It's no big deal."

Annabelle freezes. Doesn't take the car keys away from Jamie, even though he's pushing every button on the fob, and the panic alarm's going to go off any second. "Uh, yeah," she says. "I can do that. I'm pretty sure I know the ones you mean. I'll look."

She struggles Jamie into the car and, instead of starting the engine right away, pulls out her cell phone. I bet a million bucks she's calling Matt's mom to find out what brand the bagels are.

I can guarantee there'll be a pack of those bagels on the counter when I come home tonight and three more packs in the freezer. Even if she has to go to every grocery store in a fifty-kilometer radius. Even if Jamie never gets to the park.

I feel a bit guilty, but I tell myself I can pay her back by eating one in front of her later tonight. That will make her day.

Journal - Friday, August 2

▷ Do NOT want to know how many calories are in those bagels. Maybe ask Annabelle to freeze them in plain ziploc bags? No labels = no numbers.

chapter

twenty

I may not be in love with Whinny the way Matt is with Hope, but the more I get to know her, the more I respect her. She's tough, with attitude to spare, and that's what sets her apart from Hope who, even though she's not much smaller than Whinny, seems so delicate, a stiff breeze would blow her over.

Whinny's also recovering faster than the others she arrived with, her bones being covered by long, lean muscles, her coat gleaming, and her eyes and ears always swiveling, ever alert.

I've started riding her now, several times a week, while Matt watches, holding Hope on a long lead and letting her graze beside the sand ring. Hope's so fragile, sometimes even the long, fresh, untouched grass growing around the fence posts doesn't tempt her. For long periods of time, she just stands with one hip cocked, her face pressed against Matt, taking long, deep, contented breaths.

These are our quiet times, Matt's and mine, when our jobs are done and we're off the clock. Sometimes, we talk about Whinny and how she's going, but that's it; no problems, plans, or deep thoughts enter here.

"Is she tracking up for me?" I'll ask Matt.

"Not bad. Better now than at the beginning of the ride."

Our rides still consist mostly of walking—if a horse needs to be walked around here, I seem to be the one who ends up doing it—with short bursts of trot every few minutes.

My brain and body have had to accustom themselves to so many different sizes, shapes, and feelings of horses this summer. There's Bella, much wider than she should be. Slow and solid. Perfectly schooled to listen to just the right amount of leg and hand.

Then there's Sprite. Lean and muscular. He needs a strong leg and a quiet seat, and pulls like a train on the reins. The trick with Sprite is remembering not to pull back. He weighs ten times more than me and will always win a tug-of-war.

And now Whinny. She's something else altogether. Thin and whippy. It feels like I could wrap my legs right around her, and sometimes also like I might need to, the way she swerves and jumps. The key with her is to stay relaxed. She starts out at full speed, jogging along, ears flicking everywhere, waiting to be hit or yanked in the mouth or kicked.

The ultimate goal is to get her to trust me, but it requires a big leap of faith on my part first. I have to believe she won't bolt, won't take off running, won't leave me in the dust. My stomach lurches a lot, especially at the start of a ride, as she finds her rhythm and, more importantly, her confidence. As long as I keep the tension buried in my stomach, and don't let it creep into my arms or legs, or even something so small as the very tip of my baby finger, we're all right and she settles down.

It's a work in progress, but we're getting there. Now, she usually gets most of her jumpiness out within five minutes or so, and I let her reins slide long and tell myself to relax the minute I get on her back.

Tonight's going particularly well. She throws in one little experimental jog forward and, when I don't react, immediately settles down into a nice, calm walk.

"Nice work, Grace," Matt says as we pass by his spot at the fence.

Everything keeps falling into place. Whinny steps smoothly into the trot on one rein and then on the other. She keeps trotting steadily, both when I sit and when I rise. When I ask her, using my leg and seat and making a concentrated effort to hardly touch the reins, she drops quietly back to a walk and keeps moving eagerly forward.

She's learned a lot.

"She's learned a lot." It's not Matt's voice this time, it's Drew's.

I don't know how long he's been watching, but it really doesn't matter; it's all been good.

Still, just having him here changes the dynamic. I automatically want to step my show up a notch, to demonstrate how well I can do: to perform. But it's not that kind of thinking that's gotten me this far. Whinny and I have a way of doing things and, for now, at least, we need to stick to that. I take a deep breath.

"Easy," I tell myself and Whinny. We're riding past Matt at this point, and I hear him say it, too, at exactly the same time: "Easy."

I can't help giggling. Whinny's ears flick back to listen to me laugh, and then flick over to Matt because he's laughing, too, and she does a funny little sideways jig. But it's not panicked or runny—in fact, it's kind of giggly.

Drew throws his hands up. "You guys are having way too much fun," but he's smiling as he says it.

"I'm going to get out of your way and let you keep doing what you've been doing because, obviously, it's working," he says.

"ok," I say and "ok," says Matt, and we say it in unison again but manage not to giggle this time.

Before he goes, Drew pauses, looks us up and down. "If you think you're ready, I'd like to find a time when you can start riding her with me once a week."

I'm breathless. I knew we were doing well, but this is an

indication of *how* well we're doing. We wouldn't be getting any of Drew's valuable time if he didn't think Whinny was going to be worth something.

Instead of whooping for joy, I nod calmly. "Um, sure."

"Stop by the office when you've put her away," Drew says. "We'll look at the calendar."

"Wow," I say. "Wow."

I look at Matt. His eyes are shining. He smiles back at me and says it, too: "Wow."

Journal - Monday, August 5

▷ Small bathroom scale issue. Annabelle needs to weigh Jamie for passport application. Hmm … didn't anticipate that one. Staying quiet for now.

chapter

twenty-one

The barn is such a different place during the day and on weekends when everyone is off at shows. It's busy, of course it is. In some ways, it's busier than in the evenings, when all the lessons are going on and the place is bustling. During the day is when the essentials get done; mucking out stalls, unloading hay, farrier and vet visits, new horses arriving, ones who've been sold moving on.

But it's all done by us. By a core of people. Drew, Andy, Matt, Karen, Kelly, the vet, Roddy, the farrier. And, of course, this summer, me. It's rare to see anyone else around before 4:00 in the afternoon. I like it.

On the few occasions I've stayed late—to watch

Annabelle's lesson or to show a horse to a buyer that can only come later in the day—it's been strange to share the space with other people. To jostle for tack-cleaning room around the bridle hook. To wait my turn for a set of vacant cross-ties.

It's late afternoon, and I'm grooming the second of two horses I just showed to an interested buyer, when Mavis walks in. I can't remember the last time I saw her, and her appearance jolts me.

She's so skinny. She's petite, anyway, and naturally thin— I've always felt massive beside her—but this is different. Her cheeks have deflated. The scoop-neck T-shirt she's wearing reveals hollows under her collarbones. Her already small breeches bag in the butt and wrinkle around her knees.

"Take a picture, Grace; it lasts longer," she says.

So nothing else has changed, then. Mavis's personality hasn't been reduced in proportion to her body mass.

"I was just noticing ... you've lost weight." I don't know why I say it. It's a topic I normally try to avoid, but Mavis is all angles and bones. I used to believe in the saying: 'You can never be too skinny or too rich' but, for the first time ever, I wonder.

Her hands fly to her sides, smooth down the flat front of her stomach. "God, I'd hope so. Considering how *fat* I was." Her eyes narrow. "I still have a ways to go, but I can see how *to you* I'd look skinny."

If you're skinny, I'm not sure I want to get there. The words are on the tip of my tongue, but my new position as an employee here, with Mavis as a client, gives me pause. Indulging in a slanging match with her would be unprofessional. Matt walks in and saves me from the danger of letting my retort slip out. "Hey, Grace. Andy says good job with those horses. They're going to take Salem on trial."

From inside Ava's stall comes a cross between a sigh and a choke. Mavis clearly has an opinion on Matt's praise for me.

Matt ignores it. "If you don't mind waiting a bit, I can drive you home after I finish putting some gear away in the equipment shed."

"Thanks." Once he's gone, I put my horse away, sweep the aisle clear, and head into the tack room to clean my saddle and bridle.

I'm just figure-eighting my bridle, hanging it on the right peg, when Mavis steps into the room. "The aisle is a sty, Grace."

"And?" I left the aisle clean, so whatever mess is there now is somebody else's responsibility: Mavis's.

"And, I recommend you do your job and clean it up before Drew or Andy sees it. Wouldn't want to lose your sweet little job with your nice co-workers, would you?"

"Witch," I mutter to the door as it closes behind her. *Forget about her*. I roll a couple of bandages that have come loose and put them back in the proper basket. Chuck a couple of particularly dirty saddle pads in the laundry pile and step out into an extremely dirty aisle.

There's no way it could have gotten this filthy in the short time I was in the tack room, without someone working very hard at dirtying it. "Bitch!"

I grit my teeth, pick up the broom, and sweep like a crazy woman. Piles of shavings whirl across the floor and dust flies. "Sorry, guys," I say to the stall-bound horses. "I'll try to keep it down."

At the far end, I scoop my accumulated pile into a shovel, dump it in the wheelbarrow just outside the door and, when I return to put the shovel back, survey my work with satisfaction.

The aisle is spotlessly clean again. I've done an extra good job so not a stray wisp of hay or clod of dirt mars the effect. Except for the oblong directly outside Ava's stall, which is strung with wiry lengths of mane and tail hair, coated with dust, and punctuated with four piles clearly identifiable as the pickings from a horses' front and rear hooves. It stands out all the more beside the stark perfection of the rest of the aisle. *That should do it.*

As I leave the barn, Drew rushes past me. He must have been in the office, catching up on phone calls, and is now headed out to the upper sand ring to teach Mavis's lesson. My trek to the equipment shed to find Matt takes me by the ring, so I take my time, enjoy the early evening breeze, sniff the air scented with hay freshly mown in a nearby field.

"MAVIS!" Drew's distinctive voice booms with irritation.

The last thing I see, before a line of cedars obscures my sight of the ring, is Mavis, pulling Ava to a square halt. I don't mind the visual interruption, though. It means I can listen in without being seen.

"Mavis, the aisle outside Ava's stall is a complete mess. This isn't the first time you haven't swept up after yourself. I've got half a mind to send you back in there to do it."

Mavis chooses haughty over apologetic in her answer. "With the amount we pay for board, isn't that something your *staff* should do? Grace, or her little boyfriend Matt?" *Bad idea.* That isn't going to go over well with Drew.

I don't have to see Drew to know his jaw's set right now. He'll be staring Mavis down. "Excuse me?" Fingers snap. "Teachable moment! Everyone come in." Through the cedars, I can make out shapes moving from the outside of the ring, drifting toward the center.

"Where do you ride?" Drew's voice, loud and demanding. More finger snaps. "Come on, where? Anyone?"

A timid voice, uncertain—not Mavis—replies. "Stonegate?"

"Stonegate! Yes. This is not the The Royal Windsor Equestrian Club. You are not princesses. We do not have valets here. Here, at Stonegate, we groom our own horses, we clean our own tack, and we absolutely, most definitely, clean up our own messes. And if anyone thinks they pay too much board to sweep up after themselves, they can start looking for space at other stables. Understood?"

There is a chorus of "Yesses" and "Understoods," but I can't pick Mavis's voice out of the group.

The blob breaks up, with individual shapes moving back

out around the ring, when Drew speaks up again. "Oh, and Mavis? We don't spread rumors about other people's personal lives, either. Nobody cares for your gossip. Is that clear? Now bring Ava over here and I'll hold her while you go in and sweep up your mess."

Journal - Tuesday, August 6

▷ Breakfast—toast and an orange with skim milk.

▷ Lunch—Matt special: bagel, yogurt, skim milk, banana.

▷ Dinner—cottage cheese, bagel, carrot sticks, more milk.

▷ No numbers helps but the mirror's still a challenge—can't throw out all the mirrors in the house, though …

chapter

twenty-two

It's a show day. Not mine, but Iowa's first, and I get to participate as Andy's groom.

Some people might not consider this a privilege. Some people might wonder why I bothered to stay in the barn until after 10:00 PM last night after being there for hours beforehand, scrubbing manure stains and buffing hooves and braiding tiny, wiry horse hairs into a long row of submissive plaits.

Some people would shake their heads to see me rolling over on Drew and Andy's couch at 4:15 this morning, stumbling out to the barn to see how many fresh manure stains Iowa has acquired, and how many of her minute braids she's rubbed out overnight. Some people would hear this is only the beginning, and I still have a minimum of fourteen hours ahead of me, fetching and carrying food and drink for Andy and the horse, and wonder if I'm crazy.

But as I sit next to Matt in his big pickup truck, warming my hands on a steaming travel mug of lemon tea, and as the sun's rays—still so low they're almost horizontal—slice straight across me and make a little halo of dancing dust motes around Matt, I'm not bothered by my lack of sleep or the long day ahead.

We follow the trailer, eyes on the two carefully wrapped horse tails ahead of us, and we don't say anything and we don't listen to the radio. We just sit and charge our batteries for the craziness waiting for us at the end of our trip.

Hustle, bustle. Noise and movement. Everybody's maneuvering big trailers into small spaces. Everybody's walking stiff-legged horses down narrow wooden ramps. Everybody wants water and more space and more time.

Drew's voice is everywhere.

"The hunter ring's on the far side of the grounds!"

"Warm-up starts in five minutes. Not six. Five."

"Why isn't that horse saddled?"

"There's a stain right down the front of your shirt! Does anyone have a spare shirt? A *clean* spare shirt?"

Through it all, I keep my cool. Prioritize. Iowa's needs come first. Andy's second. Everyone else can wait, although, when I see Matt struggling to button his collar, I rest Iowa's saddle against the trailer and do it for him.

"Thanks," he says.

"No problem." Now back to Iowa.

I'm out of breath and have my sweatshirt tied around my waist by the time I give Iowa a last flick with my grooming cloth and watch Andy ride her off to the warm-up ring with the rest of our group.

The trailer's quiet. My tea's cold. I dump it out behind the back tire and hear a familiar voice.

"Grace?"

I stand up. "Polly!" I'm sweaty and dirty already but so is she, so I reach out and hug her. She's solid, warm. Her shoulders are broad, and I stretch my arms around them. Polly feels the way she used to look when she rode in my lesson: strong, capable and, if you were her horse, someone you wouldn't want to mess with.

"God, Grace, if you got any smaller, you'd disappear!" she says.

Over the past several months, words like this have sent pride swelling up inside me. Made me blush with pleasure and stammer out a "Thank you." Today, not so much. Partly because, rather than admiring, I might describe Polly's tone as concerned. Partly because I'm wondering if Polly's viewing me the way I viewed Mavis the other day.

"How are you?" I ask to change the subject.

"I'm good!" she says. "I've missed you. Not Stonegate so much, but you, for sure."

She doesn't miss Stonegate for a very good reason. My cheeks flush as I remember it, and I drop my gaze, pick at a piece of shaving stuck on my sleeve.

Polly was hounded from Stonegate. I don't know if he meant to but, sure as anything, Drew chased her away. He moved her onto a massive Clydesdale-cross, informing Polly—and our whole lesson—that she'd grown too heavy for her long-time favorite pony. He lurked by the dessert table at the stable Christmas party and, pointing at her plate, warned, "Unless you get some discipline, my dear, you can kiss next year's Royal goodbye."

Mavis had giggled but, for once, I felt worse than her. Because I said nothing, kept my head down, and let Polly take the heat; hoping the criticism would end with her.

I lift my eyes to meet hers. "I missed you, too. Our lesson was never as fun after you left."

Polly nods in the direction of the main show grounds. "I was just going to watch the warm-up. Want to walk over together?"

Pandemonium reigns in the warm-up ring. Hepped-up horses and nervous riders doing themselves more harm than good.

Drew's got his group in a bunch at the end, where he's talking them down, keeping them calm.

"Who're you with?" I ask Polly, and she points to a horse I know well. He's one of those horses everyone gets to know because he's so extraordinarily big—his draught-horse roots well on display—and on top of it, he always looks shaggy and a bit wild.

But he's not. He's talented. And so is the elderly lady who rides him, wearing a hunt cap that's got to be twenty-five

years old, and a show jacket someone once told me she
sewed from an old pair of curtains. I can believe it.

"So you're at Martha Turlington's place now?" I've never
been to her barn but, like everyone else, I know about the
results she gets. They compete where ribbons are awarded
based on time and points. Stay away from the hunter ring
with its heavy weighting on appearance and elegance.

"How is it?" I ask.

"I like it. It suits me."

I nod. "I'm not surprised. You're a strong rider. They're a
barn of strong riders." I admire Polly for finding a place she
fits, instead of trying to fit in somewhere she doesn't.

"How are things at Stonegate?" she asks.

"Good. Great, actually, for me. I'm working there this
summer."

At this moment, Matt rides up, holds out his crop. "Hi
Polly." His smile is broad and genuine. "Nice to see you. Can
you hold this for me, Grace?"

"Sure."

As he rides off, Polly raises her eyebrows. "Working with
Matt, by any chance?"

I can't hold back my smile.

"As a matter of fact, yes."

Polly laughs, "Well, lucky you."

Martha Turlington calls Polly over, and Andy needs me
to take Iowa while she watches the youngest riders in their
first class of the day, and the pace picks up again, and just
keeps going from there.

Which is all part of grooming. There's rarely a chance to stop because, on top of the normal ongoing maintenance of sweat to sponge from flanks and dust to flick from necks, there are always tiny crises going on, either with the rider you're grooming for or with another rider in the group. Somebody's girth strap has snapped. Someone's spilled coffee all over their cream show breeches. One of the horses is limping a bit and might be lame.

Grooms run a lot. From the stable trailer to the show office to the concession stand to the vet's trailer, and crisscrossing to and from various rings and in-gates in between. When it rains, you come home soaking down to the underwear. When it's sunny, you come home sunburned, no matter how good your intentions were to apply sunscreen all day.

Bathroom breaks, when they're taken, are on the fly. Near the end of the morning, I bolt into one of the ugly port-a-potties tucked not-so-discreetly behind a row of evergreens. As I stare in grateful relief at the back-lit green plastic ceiling, the unmistakable sounds of throwing up travel through the thin walls from the next port-a-loo over. I step out at the same time as Mavis and, like her or not, am worried enough to ask, "Are you sick?"

She scowls in reply and snaps, "Oh, grow up, Grace," and I watch the saggy backside of her retreating breeches in shocked silence.

Until I check my watch. "Oh, no!" Matt will be in the ring any minute.

I run and reach the stands out of breath, but relieved I

haven't missed Matt. There are a few riders from our barn in this class, and Matt is one of them. It's fun to see them ride, and listen to the comments of spectators around me. I know the strengths and weaknesses of each rider, and it's interesting to see whether people in the stands can pick them out as well.

Matt has a great round. The horse he's riding hates water, and I worry how they'll do at the Liverpool with its shimmering blue rectangle beneath it but, other than the slightest tail whisk, they clear it just fine. Although jumper's all about getting the job done, and not so much on how you look doing it, Matt makes it look smooth and easy, which makes watching him a real bonus.

The two giggling girls sitting in front of me are obviously enjoying watching him, too.

"So cute," one says between giggles.

"I know. Look how gorgeous his eyes are," the other one answers.

"You can hardly see his eyes from here, and that's not where I was looking, anyway."

As Matt exits the ring, he holds his reins at the buckle in one hand, shades his eyes with the other. He's scanning the stands. Looking for me? I hardly have time to wonder before he finds me and gives me a half-wave.

"Grace!" he calls. "Gracie!"

I nod. Hesitate to call back. If I do, I'll stand out; those two girls will whirl around to face me. *Oh, well. He's worth it.* "Matt!" I smile and give a big wave in response.

"Lunch?"

"OK! Meet you at the trailer after Andy's class!"

He gives me a thumbs-up and is gone to talk to Drew about his round before dismounting.

As he rides off, I'm acutely aware that the two girls are now staring at me.

Before I get up, I lean over to them and say, "I wasn't watching his eyes, either."

I smile as I pick my way out of the stands.

Journal - Saturday, August 10

▷ Ate every meal. Matt bought me a hot dog for lunch and I ate it. Plain and with no chips, but still … a hot dog!

chapter

twenty-three

Being at the show, surrounded by horses jumping everywhere, was intensely great and intensely frustrating at the same time.

Sprite's going so well. He could have out-jumped every horse there. We would have even given Matt a run for his money. I'm certain of it.

Maybe ... Maybe I should talk to Andy and Drew. Maybe they can talk to his owners. They can't possibly want to pay to board him and have me school him all summer just for him to never show at all. I could show him for free; they might win some prize money. *I'll ask Andy about it later.*

Back at the barn on Monday, it's torture to put in my time on lazy, poky Bella. At least she's cantering now—and her leg's holding up, which is great—but she's still one of the most boring horses I've ever ridden.

I'm itching to jump Sprite today. Matt will get it. I know he'll give me twenty minutes later on to chaperone our jumping session. I point my steps to Sprite's stall, just to check in—drop him a carrot—but when I get there, the stall's empty.

Unusual. But maybe the farrier's got him in the main barn. Maybe he's on special turn-out. Either way, there's no shortage of work to be done. So I move on.

I find Andy in the office. "Do you want me to ride Iowa this morning?"

"Sure." She smiles up at me from the computer monitor where she's making changes to last year's in-house show schedule, so it can be printed off for use this year. "Why don't you just hack her, though? You could probably both use some downtime."

"Thanks." A hack will be fun. The last time I was out in the woods was the day Matt and I brought the herd in. Exploring the winding trails through the trees is a perfect summer activity.

Iowa and I start off, relaxed and happy, and meander down the big hill, between the barns, past the bottom sand ring. A breeze tempers the heat of the morning sun and I'm loose, relaxed, my hips swinging along with the sway of Iowa's walk and the *crunch-crunch* of her hooves in the gravel.

We'll pass the series of small turn-out paddocks, and

then head into the big field, where the school horse herd grazes, and into the trail-laced woods beyond.

The paddocks are empty at this time of day. The horses have just come in from early turn-out, and new ones won't be put back out until later in the afternoon when the sun is lower.

A movement in one paddock, though, catches my eye. There's a horse in the far corner, where no horse should be. I stop Iowa to get a closer look.

What is that whistling sound? I shade my eyes against the rays of the morning sun. The horse has a saddle on and a rider, and the horse is Sprite.

It's the girl's father, sitting up on Sprite's back, and he has him nosed deep into the right-angled corner of the fence.

The whistling I heard is the sound of the crop as he raises it, upside down, over his head, and brings it down on Sprite's shining hide.

"There! Don't like it, do you? Nowhere for you to go now, is there?!?"

I'm afraid if I confront him, he'll simply refuse to stop. He might even turn on me. It will take me almost as long to reach the far end of the paddock as it will to dash back up the hill and get help. I'm still hesitating when Iowa decides for me.

As a slashing blow lands on Sprite's rump, Iowa jumps and spins on her back legs. When I don't fight her, she leaps forward into a canter and starts belting back the way we came.

On the way up, I see Matt's back disappearing into the tractor shed.

"Matt!" I can hardly breathe, but it's not from the ride, which is probably the shortest one I've done this year. I'm so scared, my pounding heart isn't leaving much room for my lungs to work.

Matt turns around and Drew walks up behind him.

"What is it, Grace?" Annoyance clouds Drew's face. Running green five-year-olds up steep hills is not in his training manual.

"It's Sprite!" I manage. "He's beating him. Hitting him. With his whip. Hard."

"Where?" Matt asks.

"Lower paddock!" Both he and Drew are already running in that direction when Drew calls over his shoulder. "Get Andy!" I'm relieved to have something concrete to do that doesn't involve confronting Sprite's owner. My hands are shaking, my heart is thumping, and I don't trust my own reactions right now.

"Come on, girl," I tell Iowa. "Let's go get Andy."

Very soon, it's all over. But not soon enough for Sprite. Wicked weals rise under his coat. A cut runs straight and deep across both front legs where he tried to go through the fence. The skin is split neatly—as though from a sharp knife—but underneath is a bloody mess.

Back in the barn, Matt and I flush the cut with saline solution and wait for Kelly with the antibiotics and sutures Sprite's going to need.

Last I saw of Sprite's owner, he was being escorted to the house by Drew and Andy.

"Should I have stopped it myself?"

Matt's vehement. "No! No way. You did the perfectly right thing. This way, there are witnesses, which is good."

We're both quiet for a few minutes—me smoothing ointment over Sprite's surface cuts, Matt winding support bandages on his lower legs.

"He could have hurt you, too, Grace," he adds. "And I would have hated that."

I sit with Jamie on the window seat in his room as a thunderstorm advances across the fields. It drops rain first on the neighbor's house, then their detached garage, then circles around to the east of us so, for one brief, disappointing moment, it looks like it might miss us altogether.

A heart-stopping peal of thunder cracks directly overhead and I reach for Jamie's hand, but he twitches me away, his face lit with excitement. Then the fat drops start falling and the unmistakable summer smell of hot, wet earth rises as the clouds open. The storm moves off east along the concession road, leaving in its wake a good hard summer rain.

With the excitement of the storm past, Jamie goes straight to his bed, and I follow not far behind.

The storm has carried away all the humidity of the day, leaving behind welcome fresh air. My bed is the most comfortable it's been in weeks. The sheet over my knees feels snug rather than oppressive, and nestling into the pillows is a treat.

My mind wanders back to the look on Matt's face when he said Sprite's owner could have hurt me. Just thinking about it sets up a pinched feeling inside me, one that squeezes tears to the surface. It's the same feeling I had when Matt confronted me about my eating that day in the sand ring.

As upset as I am for Sprite, it's not what happened to him that's making me cry right now. It's Matt, caring about me. Wanting to take care of me. A sob heaves out of me at the thought.

For months now, I've been trying to change—literally reshape myself—so I'll be more likable? Lovable? God, it sounds stupid put like that, and I know it's irrational, but I still can't shake this feeling that being smaller will make me more appealing.

And the thing is, it seems like Matt likes me whatever way I am.

I've made a mess, for no good reason, and I just hope I can find my way out of it.

That's enough introspection for tonight; I'm exhausted. No journaling for me.

I reach out and turn off the light and, through my dark windows, watch the final, occasional remnant of lightning streak the night sky.

chapter

twenty-four

I don't dream about the incident with Sprite specifically, but my sleep is spoiled by frequent small wakings, much tossing and turning. While I eat my puffed wheat with skim milk, and as I brush my teeth, I keep picturing Sprite forced into that corner. When I pull on my breeches, I just do them up without slipping three fingers into the waistband to see if they're tighter or looser than yesterday.

My breathing's labored as I bicycle to work; my nerves keep me from taking full, deep lungfuls of air.

As soon as I step into the barn, Andy calls out to me from the office. "Hey, Grace! Can you bed down the empty stall at the end of the aisle? There's a new horse arriving around noon."

How's Sprite? But she makes phone call after phone call, so I can't ask.

Halfway through my schooling session with Iowa, Drew calls across the ring, "If I bring you Sierra, can you pop her over a couple of fences? She refused everything she was put at last night."

How's Sprite? But Drew's on a mission. More brisk than usual. The only words he listens to when he's moving this fast are "Yes," "No," "OK," and "Sorry." Sierra jumps sweetly for me, and Drew leaves the ring, muttering about riders who ruin perfectly good horses because they have unrealistic ideas of their riding abilities.

Matt intercepts me on my way up to the back barn, which I'm starting to think of as the nursery, housing as it does all the six starved horses, a couple of school horses on stall rest and, since yesterday, Sprite.

"Hey!" he says.

"How's Sprite?"

He steps in front of me. "Hello to you, too."

"Matt ..."

"OK, sorry. I get it. Come on, walk with me and I'll tell you."

The basic answer is, nobody's sure how Sprite is. He's generally calm and he's eating, which are both very good, but his legs are badly swollen.

"Kelly says she'll have a better idea once the swelling goes down. She could x-ray but ..." Matt shrugs.

But, x-rays are expensive, and the resulting treatment

for whatever they reveal could also be very expensive. And, right now, who would pay for Sprite's treatment, anyway? Much as I'd like to know how his legs are going to be, I can see it's just as well to work on getting the swelling to go down on its own.

So I have another job now: cold water hosing Sprite's legs twice a day for twenty minutes each time. The second time I do it—right before heading home—I bring Whinny out with us and let her tear at the fresh green grass that grows around the perimeter of the wash stall.

At the beginning of the summer, who would have guessed that the favorite part of my day wouldn't be schooling Iowa for her next show, or riding the huge, ridiculously expensive flea-bitten grey Drew's considering recommending to one of his adult riders, but standing around, babysitting two somewhat damaged horses in long-term recovery?

Not me. I thought I loved jumping Sprite, but maybe I just love Sprite, period. All I know is, I wouldn't trade these two horses for the world.

I check my watch. Our twenty minutes are up. "Come on! Invalids back to the barn."

◆ ◆ ◆

Annabelle's car is gone and the house is quiet when I get home. *Nice.* I've just about decided to take the day off from running and maybe have a bath before eating my new ritual dinner. For the past several nights, it's been cottage cheese with carrot and celery sticks and one of Matt's famous raisin and cinnamon thin bagels.

It's a weird meal, but I eat it at the table with Annabelle and Jamie, and Annabelle never says a word. Whenever I go through one tub of cottage cheese, there's another in the fridge, so I'm assuming she approves.

I would never admit it, but I look forward to this meal, and I'm surprised how relaxing it is to just sit down and eat rather than keeping several plausible-sounding lies at the ready to help me avoid it.

I'm padding through the front hall in my riding socks, wondering if maybe I should toast my bagel tonight, when an envelope on the table catches my eye.

Creamy white with a Manchester postmark in the top right-hand corner. Why is my dad writing a letter to Annabelle on such expensive, fancy—formal—stationary? This can't be good. I hold it up to the light, smooth the paper flat as I can, trying desperately to read what's inside. No hope.

Maybe it's fine. Maybe he's been nominated for the Nobel Prize. OK, I doubt that, but maybe it's some big announcement. A good one.

My stomach churns. So much for taking the day off; I have to run or I'll explode. As for dinner ... well, right now, the thought of eating makes me sick.

Ten minutes later and I'm struggling to keep my cadence steady. All it takes is a mental image of that envelope to spike my heart rate, send my breathing quick and shallow, and unleash a swarm of butterflies in my insides.

Don't think about it. Breathe in, breathe out. Find your pace.

Finally, I do. My heart, stomach, lungs all return to normal functioning, and my pulse pumps in its standard running mode, elevated but not racing. The rhythms of my run soothe me, the blood whooshing through my ears, feet crunching through the gravel, and ponytail swish-swishing across the back of my neck.

My run has done what I needed it to. Settled my nerves— and my stomach—just enough to re-shape *I'm too upset to eat*, into, *I need some food to steady me*. Whatever's written in that letter isn't going to be changed by what I do or don't eat.

◆ ◆ ◆

When I come down from my post-run shower, Annabelle and Jamie are home and the letter's gone. So Annabelle's seen it. I wait for her reaction but, on the surface, there is none. So there goes the Nobel Prize theory. I'm pretty sure she would have shared that kind of major news with Jamie and me.

I've rarely seen her so distracted. She moves through dinner on autopilot. Had I wanted to, it would have been a good night for me to skip dinner, since Annabelle isn't really paying attention, anyway. I have to fetch Jamie's yogurt and his milk from where she's forgotten them on the counter beside the fridge. She picks at her own food, and doesn't insist on Jamie's eating any of his cut-up veggies before she slips him a chocolate chip cookie.

When she reappears in the family room after tucking Jamie into bed, there's a forced casualness in her voice. "So, you just going to read tonight?"

I look up from the Dick Francis paperback I'm re-reading for the third time and shrug. "Probably."

"'Kay then!" And she's gone. But I know where she'll be.

Sure enough, when I use my first excuse to travel by my dad's office (heading upstairs to swap my shorts for yoga pants), the door's almost completely closed, with light slicing out onto the hardwood floor of the hallway.

The next time I walk by (seeking a scrunchie to ponytail my hair), the door's pulled to. Annabelle's voice, muffled, rises and falls inside and, back in the kitchen, the "in use" light glows red on the cordless phone base.

My final patrol is the one taking me upstairs and to bed. The closed door gives nothing away. What should I do? I always say goodnight to Annabelle. It's one of the basic routines of our household. My nerves send my left fingers snaking around my right wrist, something I realize I haven't done much lately. I take a deep breath, knock, and quickly push the door inward, just a crack.

Annabelle's on the phone, nodding, making notes. She raises her face to me and smiles, but her worried eyes don't match her upturned lips.

"'Night," I whisper.

'Night, she mouths in return, pointing at the receiver and making an apologetic face.

I climb into bed, not at all reassured, but my sleep deprivation takes over and I don't remember much after my head hits the pillow.

I'm woken by what? It must be Annabelle coming to bed. I crane my neck and twist my head to squint at the clock radio beside my bed. After midnight. It's unlike Annabelle to be up at this hour.

Then, *scrape-click*, the telltale noise of the chain on Annabelle's bedside lamp—switching it off—travels down the hall.

Now I can't sleep again. I stare at the crisscross patterns the moon, filtered by the tree outside, throws on my quilt. I flex every muscle in my body, then relax them one at a time. My version of counting sheep. But it doesn't work.

The heel-toe, heel-toe of my bare feet on hardwood is all but soundless as I creep down the hall. As I try to avoid the particularly creaky steps, I set off a couple of other smaller squeaks, but nothing that should wake Annabelle or Jamie.

And then I'm on the ground floor, and the doorway to the office is just ahead and off to the right, and a rush of adrenaline surges through me, dizzying me. I'm going, though; I've already decided. Four long strides and I'm at the door. It's not even closed, which makes me feel a little better. Two steps take me to the desktop—clear in the middle with neat piles around the outside.

For some reason, it feels OK to read the letter but not OK to rifle through everything on the desk. Even though I no longer feel his presence anywhere in the house—Annabelle's rearranged her clothes to take over his side of the closet, and we no longer have British beers and marmite in the fridge—the office remains my dad's territory and, even with him an ocean and five hours away, I don't want to touch any papers he might have left here. I think back to my "goodnight" to Annabelle—picture her sitting here, holding the telephone, writing on a pad of paper—what was in front of her?

A blue folder. I'm positive because blue is Jamie's favorite color these days and, subconsciously, I linked Jamie to that folder. A blue folder sits right on top of the front left-hand pile. I hold my breath, ease the top flap open with the fingernail on my index finger and ... *voila*! Thick ivory paper. My dad's name centered at the top in neat typed font. My dad's signature scrawled at the bottom in illegible splotchy pen.

Dear Annabelle:

While I have not asked my solicitor to write this letter, I have consulted with him with regard to its contents. Accordingly, I would ask you to take this correspondence seriously.

I am troubled by the reports I have received, from

Dr. Leonora Keelor, of Grace's anorexia and its progression over the summer.

I am willing to admit my responsibility in this for not realizing the seriousness of the situation sooner. I also feel I may have put too much responsibility on your shoulders. Caring for our son is a considerable amount of work on its own; however, you are also faced with the needs of a troubled teenager who is not even related to you.

I have a proposal, which I believe will be in the best interests of all concerned. A colleague here at the university has recommended a boarding school specializing in teens with eating disorders. Sending Grace to this school will get her the help she needs, relieve you of the burden of her care, and the cost will be covered by my benefits package at the university.

Oh. My. God.

I have made inquiries, and the school is currently holding a place for Grace, beginning in September. It is located in the countryside, approximately one hour from Manchester, and I feel sure she will enjoy it. She can fly here, to Manchester, and I will drive her to the school for the start of classes.

I understand there are some logistics to be handled. I will, of course, pay for Grace's passport and other expenses associated with her travel.

I would ask that you begin making the necessary arrangements to ensure she can fly to the UK by September 7.

Sincerely,

Doug Madden
cc. James Hooper, Hooper Wollen Solicitors

OhMyGod, OhMyGod, OhMyGod.
This is wrong. This is so wrong. There are at least seventeen ways this is wrong. Or maybe seventeen *million*.

I need to talk to Matt. I need to talk to my dad. Look at the clock. Both are impossible. Plus, I would never, in a million years, know what to say to my dad. He baffles me. I hardly know him. *I hate him.*

I need to run. To bike. To ride a horse. A horse as tough as Sprite, who will fight me and try to run away with me and focus my mind on nothing but *him.*

I press my face against the window. It's pitch black. The wind is moaning. It's started raining and drops spatter the window. It's horrible out there.

What to do?

Warm milk. Hard to believe food could provide a solution

right now. I pour a mug, pop it into the microwave. *If only my dad—Doug—could see me now. Look, Dad: I'm eating!* I laugh a low, bitter laugh.

I spend the two minutes it takes the drink to warm, pacing. Around and around the kitchen island. Back and forth from the stove to the fridge. Finally, just shifting from foot to foot in front of the microwave, like a horse that came to the barn on trial and we sent away because of his incessant weaving, not wanting him to pass his bad habit on to the others.

Ping!

The first sip burns my mouth. The pain feels right alongside my anger, which balloons now. Bigger and bigger, taking up all the space inside me. I fumble my way into the garage, close the insulated door to the house tight behind me. The concrete's cold and smooth under my feet, and the fluorescent strips bathe everything in an eerie, sinister light.

I scream. Let loose. Yell until my lungs are empty and my throat is raw. I let it all out.

And when, exhausted, I'm done, I'm amazed to find I'm still holding the steaming skim milk—now just the right temperature—without a drop spilled.

I take a tentative sip. *Mmm.* Warm. Bland, in a comforting way.

Annabelle's voice, *This'll make you sleepy. There's nothing like warm milk.* Annabelle. I wish I could talk to her. But this is all too much right now. And if she's managed to fall asleep, I don't want to wake her up.

Plus, there's that little line in the letter I can't forget: "A troubled teenager who is not even related to you." I don't think that's the way she sees me. Then again, until five minutes ago, I would never have seen myself in a boarding school for anorectics in middle-of-nowhere England. Maybe I'm stupid. Maybe I don't see things I should.

Maybe I should have been easier to live with. Maybe I should have stopped pushing back when all Annabelle wanted was for me to eat.

I used to be horrified at the thought of my anorexia robbing me of riding. Now it seems like I have much, much more to lose.

I can't talk to Annabelle until I figure some stuff out.

Journal - Tuesday, August 13

▷ Only twenty-five days till September 7 …

chapter

twenty-five

I've barely seen Matt today and, while it's not unusual for us to have different tasks during the day, I would have expected him to take a few seconds to stop by while I hosed Sprite's leg, or to lean on the fence for a minute while I schooled Iowa.

Hope's off her feed, which is a bad sign in any horse, but dangerous for one still so undernourished. The vet, here to check on other horses, spent a few minutes with her, but didn't come to any particular conclusion.

When I asked Andy, "Is Hope ok?" she shrugged and sighed.

"Kelly took some blood. We'll see."

At the end of the day, Matt seeks me out in my usual

spot at Whinny's stall, with a grim face and the usual light missing from his eyes. I'm almost surprised when he asks me to go to the field with him. I would have guessed he'd rather be alone.

But, "Sure," I say. "Great." Partly because I'd take any opportunity to spend time with Matt, and partly because he soothes me and, after reading my dad's letter, I could use some soothing.

I've spent my day torn between telling myself it can't be true, and it'll never happen, and reminding myself I read it with my own eyes. *September 7. Less than a month away. Don't think about it.*

Matt doesn't say a word to me on the drive to the field, and I can't figure out how to start the conversation.

He parks in the usual spot, and I wait for him to hop around to the back of the pickup and pull out the scythe and the burlap sack he uses for the grass he cuts for Hope.

Instead, he steps out of the truck and walks over to lean on the fence.

I step up beside him, place my hand on his arm. "Aren't you going to cut grass?"

He twitches away from me. "What's the point, Grace? She's not eating."

"Well, if she'll eat anything, she'll eat this grass."

"And what if she doesn't? What if she won't? Maybe I don't want to find out."

I shrug. "Suit yourself." I get it. Sort of. There are things I don't want to find out, either. But we have to try. I have to try.

Three minutes later, I'm hip-deep in the grass, hacking away at it. Half of everything I try to stuff in the sack falls out again, but I'm determined.

I imagine the first clump of grass is my dad's letter. *Whack!* That one is the stupid, stupid boarding school. *Slash!* And this is for my dad's completely ignoring me, except when he wants to take over my life. *Slam! Thud!* "Crap!"

The blade of the scythe is stuck fast, lodged several inches into the sun-dried earth of the field.

I'm bent over, examining it, when a shadow blocks the sun from my face. Matt's shadow. "Need some help?"

"Only if you think it's worth your while."

"It might be." He reaches down, grabs the handle of the tool with two hands and maneuvers it free. "I think I'll use this now, before you kill someone."

Matt fills the remaining three-quarters of the sack in half the time I spent on the first quarter. He heaves it into the back of the truck, then comes to sit next to me in the shade under the tree.

His face lightened while he cut the grass, but he's gone tense again.

"What's wrong?"

"Don't be stupid, Grace."

"Ouch! Sorry for asking."

"I'm pissed off. ok? Good enough answer for you?"

"At who?" I half-expect another 'Don't be stupid.'

Instead, Matt says, "I think Hope's going to die."

I shake my head. "She is *not*. Don't say that."

"She is, Grace. There's a really good chance of it. When animals—horses, people—don't eat, they die. And with Hope, it's not her fault. She didn't want to be starved, but you've done it to yourself, and it pisses me off."

I couldn't be more winded if he'd punched me in the gut. I can't find my breath. Can't take in oxygen. My throat aches with a horrific constriction. I put one hand to my neck, raise the other in the air, palm forward, and concentrate on drawing just one breath.

"Are you OK?" He leans forward, hands spread like he wants to help but doesn't know how.

I blink, bite my lip, manage one deep inhale through my nose, then out again. It calms me enough to let me protest. "It's not like that."

He settles back. Crosses his arms across his chest. "Then, what is it like?"

I search for the words Dr. Keelor, at two hundred dollars an hour, has never been able to pull from me. My eye falls on the truck parked just a few meters away. "It's like the mirror on your truck," I say. "You know, 'OBJECTS IN MIRROR ARE CLOSER THAN THEY APPEAR.' Except for me, it's 'Objects in mirror appear larger than they are.'

"I started feeling terrible about myself. I felt huge. I couldn't stand myself; I couldn't imagine how anyone else could stand me. So, I lost five pounds—I thought it would help—and then I thought it would be better to have another five pounds off as a buffer. Just in case. I didn't plan for it to get as bad as it did." I look away, across the field, then look back at him. "I regret it. If that helps. I really do." If only he knew how much. As badly as I want to tell him about my dad's threat, right now it would be too much. I'll tell him soon. If he's still talking to me ...

"So, if you regret it, why are you still doing it? You're still so thin." He holds his voice steady. His brow is less furrowed. But his question suggests his anger remains.

"I'm not. Not as much. I got into it gradually and I need to undo it gradually. I've started." I pause. Try a half-smile. "*You* started me, actually."

"I did?"

"You did. You with your 'I'll tell Annabelle' and 'I'll tell Drew' and 'I'll help you jump Sprite.' You with your super-addictive raisin cinnamon bagels."

I haven't cried through all this, but the tears are brimming now. I sniff. "Because I like you. I really, really like you." *Keep trying.* "More than I've ever liked anyone else before."

Matt's leaning close to me and I lean closer to him, and now I know why the first thing you do when you meet a strange horse is exchange breaths with them. It's an inexplicable thing, how another living thing's warm breath can create such cold shivers, but I'm shivering as I wait for Matt to touch me.

He swallows, so hard I can hear it, and he straightens up and gets to his feet. "I'd better be getting you home."

Five minutes later, I'm standing in my driveway holding

onto my bike, saying, "Thanks for the ride."

I contemplate the mess my life is in. The guy I thought was going to kiss me didn't. But, hey, who cares? Because I might be gone in a few short weeks, anyway. In addition to never seeing Matt again, I may never live with Annabelle again, never ride Whinny or Sprite or Iowa again—who knows if I'll even be able to ride at all for the foreseeable future? Oh, and don't forget Jamie. Maybe once he's my age, I'll be able to visit him a couple of times a year.

And I have about twenty pounds to gain. So what's the logical next step? I run.

I run and I run and I run, in an effort to let the *slap-slap* of my footfalls, and the *out-out-in* of my breathing, and the *swish-swish* of my ponytail, dull the panic rising in me. It might be counterintuitive, but it's the only way I'm going to be calm enough to eat my dinner, and the one thing I know for sure is that if I have any hope of not getting on a plane to Manchester at the beginning of September, I'm going to need to eat every meal between now and then.

Journal - Wednesday, August 14

▷ Twenty-four days and counting.

chapter
twenty-six

Oh, bliss, oh, joy. Dr. Keelor's back from holidays and she's gearing up for another anti-riding discussion with Annabelle. She begins with, "Do you feel Grace's riding has contributed to her anorexia?" and, before Annabelle can answer, hands her a massive stack of paper. "Were you aware that a number of studies have found a correlation between horseback riding and eating disorders?"

"You mean, like the studies that show a link between eating disorders and boarding schools?" They both stare at me. Dr. Keelor's knuckles whiten as she grips her clipboard.

"Like the boarding school my dad wants to send me to? According to Google, it'll be perfect. I can hide all my food and, if I feel like it, I can even take up puking after meals and nobody'll notice. Except all the other girls, who'll be doing it, too. Sounds great. Sign me up."

I can't look at Annabelle. This isn't the way I wanted to bring this up. But I've started and I'm not backing down. Instead, I hold Dr. Keelor's gaze—dare her to say something, *will* her to say something. Bring it on. I'm ready.

She sighs. "Really, Grace, I don't think *Google* is the best place to gather information." Then dismisses me completely by turning back to Annabelle. "So, Grace is still riding?"

Annabelle nods. "Riding, yes." Then, with a sideways glance my way, "And eating dinner with us every night."

Thank you, Annabelle.

Dr. Keelor's lips pucker as she pushes them together. "Hmmm ..." She turns to a fresh page on her clipboard. "Let's talk about something new."

This should be good. What study is she going to trot out now?

"Let's talk about your family history."

Annabelle and I straighten at the exact same time. The chrome frame of the leather couch creaks at the sudden weight shift.

"What about it?" Annabelle says.

"Well, for a start, you live with your stepmother," she indicates Annabelle, "and your stepbrother." I liked it better when she was talking about studies.

I shake my head. "He's my brother."

Again with the pursed lips, as she glances down at

something on her clipboard. "Your half-brother, I believe." Emphasis on the *half*.

When neither Annabelle nor I reply, she continues. "And the reason you live with your step-family is due to the mental illness of your mother, which ultimately led to her death. Is that right?"

"No! I ... uh ... she ..."

"Who told you that!" There's fury, white hot, in the steel of Annabelle's voice. "*I* am paying you, so if you've been talking to my estranged husband, I'd like an explanation as to why!"

I don't hear the explanation. I'm gone. So fast, neither of them tries to stop me. I push through the heavy wooden door, cross the empty waiting room in seconds, and am out in the hospital corridor.

My eyes fly to a red "Exit" sign and I follow them. I end up in a zigzagging stairway. Take the steps two at a time to a huge steel door. Lunge against the exit bar and stumble out to grass—weedy, but green—and sky—overcast, but welcome. The door clicks shut behind me and I suck in fresh outdoor air.

I want to run. Home, preferably. Settle instead on walking. Fast. Laps around the parking lot. Balancing on the curbs, falling off where they're crumbled.

"Grace?"

I whirl around. Annabelle. Arms open, palms up. Creating a space that will fit me perfectly.

"Annabelle ..." I walk into her, pull my arms up tight

between us, let her do all the hugging—all the holding—smush my face into her shoulder and mumble, "What is my dad *doing*?"

"You know."

I raise my face so I can breathe. So I can answer. "About the letter? Yes. I saw it when it came. I read it when you were in bed."

She nods. "I figured. When I searched for the boarding school, the site was already highlighted."

I push back so I can look her properly in the eye. "I'm so sorry it got to this, Annabelle. I'm trying, you know. I really am."

"I know you are, baby." The "baby" undoes me. Sobs rise in me.

"Jamie's your baby." The last word comes out long and interrupted with a hiccup.

"You've been in my life since you were a baby. You're just as much mine as Jamie is. Nothing your dad or the doctor or anybody else says can change that."

"Can he take me away? Will they let him?"

"I'm fighting it, Grace. I'm trying, too. I'm doing research, getting advice. If we try together, we'll have a better chance."

"I'll keep trying. I promise. I'll do anything."

She puts her arm around me and tugs me back toward her. "For right now, all you have to do is get in the car and come home with me and have a decent lunch. Not a big lunch—just a nutritious one—and then we'll figure things out, one step at a time."

As we drive out of the parking lot, and Annabelle pays the cheerful attendant, he calls, "See you next time!"

I shudder. *Oh, God, I hope not.*

♦ ♦ ♦

When Annabelle and I walk into the house, Jamie jumps up from where he's sitting with his babysitter, doing one of his favorite puzzles for the eighty-seventh time. He runs to us and head butts first me then Annabelle.

She lifts him up to kiss his cheek. "Where'd you get this cap, buddy?" He has a familiar-looking cap on, worn and red, with the leather strap at the back cinched in tight to hold it on Jamie's small head.

"Matt gave it to me," he says, putting one hand on his head and smiling broadly.

My insides clench. I swallow hard.

"Matt?" Annabelle asks and looks at me, eyebrows raised. I shrug.

"Oh, yes," says Jamie's babysitter. "Grace's friend Matt came by to drop something off. He left it in your room," she says, looking at me. "I hope that was OK. And Jamie liked his cap, so he let him keep it."

I'm halfway up the stairs before she finishes her sentence.

In my room, nothing. I don't even know what I'm looking for, but figure anything new should stand out in the familiar surroundings. But no, my bed: made. Desk: unusually tidy. Chair: covered with clothes but nothing else.

The mirror. My gaze flicks over it, then sticks. A note,

tucked into the frame, bears ten simple block-printed words: "OBJECTS IN MIRROR ARE MUCH MORE BEAUTIFUL THAN THEY APPEAR."

♦ ♦ ♦

I spend my afternoon mucking, sweeping, raking, and more sweeping—the jobs Matt normally does, because Matt's spending the afternoon out in the field with Drew and the tractor and Ken Scott (the groundhog shooter), and they're digging, and hauling, and hammering, and screwing two big new cross-country jumps together.

As I'm stirring up a bran mash for Hope—building on the positive sign of her eating all the grass we cut in the field yesterday—the tractor revs particularly loudly and shouts drift up the hill.

Andy, walking by, rolls her eyes and says, "Men!" but I'm feeling kindly toward one of the men down there, so I just smile and shrug.

Andy's smiling later, too, when she calls me into the office and points to a thermos and a stack of cups. "I made lemonade to take to the guys, but I thought you might want some first."

"I could take it for you." I step forward, reach my hand out to the thermos.

She holds up her hand. "It's OK, I actually called you in here to talk to you. Can you sit down for a minute?"

"Of course." I perch on the hard step-stool that doubles as a platform for braiding manes on the night before shows.

Andy is softer, kinder, more personable than Drew. I feel more at ease with her. But sitting, waiting for her to talk, is still nerve-wracking. I'm glad of the cup of lemonade she hands me. I can't fidget while I hold it.

"First of all, let me say, I haven't talked to Annabelle about this, and I'm not sure if I should have, but I've been impressed by your responsibility and common sense this summer, so I'm just going to go ahead and talk to you."

OK, so this sounds major.

"It's about Sprite."

I don't know if I can handle another Sprite discussion. Starting with my dad and moving to Drew, they haven't gone particularly well for me. I'm cautious as I nod. "OK."

"You've been doing great work with him."

Is this where she says something nice before saying something terrible? "Thank you."

"He was a challenge to us. We were relieved when the Osments bought him."

I shudder at the mention of their name, and Andy nods. "Well, yes, that didn't work out so well. Without going into details, we've taken back ownership of Sprite, which means we once again have a difficult horse that not many of our students can ride on our hands, along with a fair whack of vet bills. And he's going to rack up more before he's completely sound." She pauses. "*If* he ends up being completely sound, which we hope he will but, as you know, there are no guarantees."

I nod. I understand. I don't know where I fit in all this.

"Drew and I would like you to have him."

I lean back and nearly fall off the stool.

"Our proposal is for you to pay for his current vet bills and we'd sign him over to you. Obviously, there's a lot to consider, in terms of his injury and what it will cost to keep him from now on. You'll need to talk to Annabelle, and you'll want to get Kelly's opinion."

I'm speechless. I sit and stare at her.

"You don't know what to say, do you?"

I shake my head.

She laughs. Comes out from behind the desk. Hugs me. "It's OK. Let it sink in. Think about it. Sleep on it."

I finally stammer out an answer. "I'm interested."

"I know you are." She juggles the cups and the thermos into a worn cloth bag.

"I really love him."

"We know you do, Grace."

I follow her out of the barn. Blink in the bright sunlight. Sprite could be mine. *Sprite.*

Journal - Thursday, August 15

▷ Kept my promise to Annabelle. Ate lunch. Even drank a cup of lemonade. Will keep trying. For me, for Matt, for Annabelle, for SPRITE!

chapter
twenty-seven

I'm snugging Whinny's girth up, laughing as she gnashes her teeth in protest, when Drew walks around the corner.

I jump, "Oh!" The standing stalls are my territory. And Matt's. And the skinny horses we take care of.

"What?" Drew asks.

I shake my head. "Nothing. Sorry. Do you need me for something?"

He points at Whinny, snaps his fingers. "I need her."

"Whinny?"

He nods. "Bring her to the bottom sand ring. I'm going to ride her."

I pace tiny circles in the middle of the sand ring. I don't

know where to stand. Don't know what to do with my hands. Drew is on my horse.

Whinny takes two mincing steps sideways. Drew shifts his weight and settles himself in the saddle. Her ears flick back, then front again, and she drops her head down, accepts the bit, and walks steadily forward. She's the picture of calm, graceful relaxation.

How does he do in thirty seconds what I'm still working on after weeks of schooling her?

Who cares? Look at her trot! In a perfect frame, neck arched, tracking up beautifully, tail held with pride. She's gorgeous.

Drew is still and strong on her back. He gives her the aid to change reins, but I can't see it. He asks her to canter—a beautiful balanced canter—but without a visible outward sign.

I'll never ride like Drew—that's a given—but it's a treat to watch him. And to see Whinny respond to his quiet confidence, his lifetime of experience.

He brings her to a halt beside me, smooth and square. Instead of yanking the reins away and dropping her head to her knees, Whinny remains alert, mouthing the bit, ears pricked forward.

I stand equally alert and await Drew's verdict.

"You've done great work with this mare. She's far better than I expected. Move her into the schooling barn; there are some lessons I want to use her in."

My breath catches, makes a small hiccupping noise. Stay

calm. "OK, I can do that."

"Grace?"

"Yes?"

"Don't be so surprised. You have talent."

You have talent. Talent. I'm walking up the hill beside Drew and Whinny, letting the words run through my head, soaking them in, enjoying them, when Andy appears, half-jogging, around the bend.

"Grace! I need you."

I glance at Drew. "Go. I'll put her away. You can pick a new stall for her later."

I barely have time to say "OK, thanks!" before Andy's linked her arm in mine and is pulling me toward the main barn.

"There are people here to look at Iowa."

"OK ..."

"These aren't just any people, Grace. These are people with *serious* buying power."

"OK." We detour around a massive vehicle blocking our path to the barn. "Is that a Hummer?"

"Mm-hmm." Andy nods her head toward the personalized license plate. It bears an NHL logo and reads, "JCT."

I gasp. "Oh, my God, is J.C. Trottier here?"

Andy nods harder and my brain keeps racing. "Is *J.C. Trottier* looking at Iowa?"

"For his daughter," Andy confirms as she drags me into the barn, points to where Matt's grooming a cross-tied Iowa. "Matt will fill you in. I've got to schmooze."

My knees and stomach both wobble while my brain fizzes: *I* could convince J.C. Trottier to buy Iowa for his horse-crazy daughter. Also, I could completely *blow* this and send J.C. Trottier off to another stable.

Matt saddles Iowa and bridles her. Fishes a tiny pair of scissors out of his pocket and trims a few too-long whiskers. Meanwhile, I brush the same chunk of her tail over and over and over again.

While Matt works, he talks. "Their daughter's twelve— you know that, right?"

"*Their* daughter?"

"His wife's here, too."

"Wow." I wonder if she's as in-your-face pretty as she always looks in magazines and newspapers.

"The daughter's name is ..."

"Hayley." At least a small part of my brain is still functioning.

"She's growing out of her pony, and they want to buy her a horse for her birthday. They want it to be a surprise. That's why they want you to ride her—they want to see a girl about her size on the horse."

With Iowa gleaming and ready, he steps over to me. "Come here. Andy brought a bunch of her stuff for you." He hands me a velvet hunt cap and, while I have my hands up, adjusting the harness, he starts threading a belt through the loops of my breeches.

Oh, my God. Not only do I have to ride a horse for Mr. and Mrs. Big-Shot NHL, but Matt is touching me. His hands feed the leather along my front, then my side. When he reaches the back, he has to put both hands around me— one to pass the belt through the loop, the other to receive it. He's so close I can feel his body heat. We both turn our heads at the same time and my hot cheek grazes his slightly scratchy one.

"Sorry."

"It's fine." I say it on an exhale, and the words sound as weak as my knees feel.

"Matt! Grace!" Andy strides down the aisle. "Are you ready?" She doesn't wait for an answer. "She looks good." I don't know if she means me or Iowa.

Andy leans forward, smoothes a stray piece of hair under my helmet. "You haven't had your birthday yet, right, Grace?"

"I, uh, no." Matt's crouching beside me, wiping dust off my boots. "It's on the twenty-second."

"Friday? Good. I told them you were fifteen; the younger the better, I think."

She steps back, gives two sharp nods, and says, "Let's go sell this mare."

"It's fine. It's no big deal. You can do it." Matt whispers as he legs me up onto Iowa.

In the background, Andy's already talking. "As you can see, she stands very quietly for mounting." She raises her voice. "You can just warm her up like normal, Grace. Give Mr. and Mrs. Trottier a chance to watch her for a few minutes."

Mrs. Trottier laughs. "Please, just call me Genevieve!" I sneak a look at her. She's as pretty as in her pictures and seems as friendly as the newspapers always say she is. Thank goodness for that.

Iowa walks forward energetically, just the way we've taught her to. She flexes slightly to the inside and bends nicely around her corners.

She moves into trot without hesitation and back down to walk without a fight.

When Andy asks me to canter her, she picks up the correct lead on both reins.

"Try a simple change with her," Andy says, and she does that perfectly, as well.

"We've been working on that with her just recently," Andy tells the couple. "She learns very quickly."

"Great. So, can we see her jump?" It's funny to hear a voice I've heard a dozen times on radio sportscasts and *Hockey Night in Canada* here, talking about a horse I'm riding.

Or, at least, it would be funny if he didn't want me to jump her. Because Iowa doesn't really do that yet. Oh sure, we've been working with raised ground poles and tiny cavaletti—at most, a foot high—but we haven't actually *jumped* her.

"Of course," says Andy. "Let me just set something up. Grace, why don't you give Iowa a breather while I do this?"

It seems natural to ride her toward the couple who might buy her, so I walk in their direction. Where J.C. looks interested, Genevieve is eager. She steps through the rails of the fence and walks to Iowa, hand outstretched.

"Hi pretty girl," she croons. Iowa whiffles gently at her palm.

"She likes to have her ears scratched," I offer.

Genevieve's fingers find Iowa's ears and, sure enough, the mare drops her head down and gives a deep groan. Genevieve laughs. "She's charming!"

I nod. "She really is. She's a pleasure to work with."

"We need to find just the right horse for Hayley. She loves Pumpkin so much, but he's far too small for her these days."

"Iowa's got quite a personality." It's Andy, back from jump-building.

Genevieve sighs. "She's lovely. It makes me think maybe I should get back into riding myself."

Andy looks at me, raises one eyebrow, then turns to Genevieve. "Well, if you decide to do that, we certainly have some other horses we could show you. Now, would you like to watch her jump from in here?" She nods at me to take Iowa back out on the rail.

Great. Fine. No pressure. Now Andy and Drew might be selling *two* horses to this family. All I have to do is take a mare that's never jumped over a few rails.

In the center of the ring, Andy's telling Genevieve, "Oh, yes, she's a great little rider." A great rider would get this done. I gather up my reins, ask Iowa to trot, and decide to do whatever Andy asks me.

"First, over the cavaletti, just to warm up!"

Put impulsion into the trot, hold just enough contact to guide Iowa without restricting her, show her the low pole, and let her hop over it. Easy. Fine. Done.

"Now over the "x," Grace!"

OK, same thing. Don't worry. Circle in a nice forward trot, give her a good few strides to suss out the jump. Concentrate on the rhythm of my breathing and the pattern of Iowa's hoofs, and ride forward like there's nothing in front of us.

Iowa takes a huge, careful, rounded leap and clears the jump with a foot to spare. *Shoulders back! Chest open! Don't catch her in the mouth!*

We land and she snorts with pleasure and gives a little skip that's more polite than a buck, and I laugh and pat her on the neck and call out to Andy, "What next?"

Matt drops our lunch in front of me and swings his legs under the table. The grin on his face swells my heart. *God, he's gorgeous.*

"You're amazing. You're a genius. They're buying her."

"They are?"

"And coming back to look at horses for Genevieve next week."

"Really?"

"*And* talking about keeping Iowa here, and both Hayley and Genevieve riding here."

"*Really?* Wow!"

"You're wow."

I blush, finger a knot in the tabletop, hold his gaze for a second before blushing more deeply and dropping it again. "Are you going to feed me, or what?"

"I am, but ... look at me, Grace." I keep my head angled down so just my eyes peek up at him. "I'm serious, Grace, don't look away."

"ok." I straighten up, face him squarely. His cheeks are flushed, too. "What?"

"I was wondering ..." he pauses, clears his throat. "I was wondering if you'd go out with me?"

My breath disappears. "Out?"

"For your birthday."

"My birthday?"

"You told Andy it's on Friday. I mean, I totally get it if you have plans." He rubs his forehead. "Actually, I'm a total idiot. You probably do have plans. I mean, you're turning sixteen—it's kind of a big deal—so, if you do, I'm sorry ..."

"No!"

"No?" His shoulders drop.

"I mean, no, you're not an idiot. At all. No, I don't have plans. Except with you. If you really mean it."

"I really mean it."

"Wow. ok. Great."

What a day, what a day, what a day. Whinny graduating into lessons. Iowa sold. Matt asking me out. *Matt asking me out!*

"Did you bring me a bagel? I'm starving!"

Journal - Wednesday, August 21

▷ Annabelle found me a new therapist. Says she's nice, young, used to ride. "You'll like her." Will try to. Am hopeful.

▷ Going to try giving the journal a rest for a while …

chapter

twenty-eight

I burst into the kitchen, sweaty from the breakneck pace of my bike ride home, filthy from my long day's work at the barn, and panicking because Matt's picking me up in forty-five minutes.

Annabelle intercepts me. "Where have you been? You need to go in less than an hour!"

"I was getting ready to leave when Andy said I could ride Sprite—I couldn't resist."

Annabelle shakes her head. Hands me a plate with a bagel toasted golden-brown lying on it. "Get in the shower and you can eat this while I dry your hair."

When I don't move fast enough, she puts her hands on my shoulders, pushes me toward the stairs. "Go, now! I want to hear the water running in thirty seconds."

Nineteen minutes later, I'm sitting on the closed toilet lid with my head upside down between my legs, while Annabelle blows hot air through my hair.

Every now and then, I tap her leg, and she lets me lift my head so I can swallow chewed bits of bagel.

Finally, the hair dryer shuts off and, into the sudden silence, she says, "Voila! Witness the perfection." Hasn't even finished the "n" sound in "perfection" when the doorbell rings.

"I'll get it!" And she's gone, leaving me alone to check myself out in the mirror. I choose the full-length one in my room, the one still holding Matt's message. I keep my eyes shut as I step in front of it. Count down in my head and open them up, and am shocked by what I see.

Not me. Really, it isn't. My hair's not tied back in a practical ponytail or twisted up in a clip. Instead, it's bouncy and shiny, and I can't believe how long it's grown. It spills down my back and over my shoulders. I had to turn down the tank top Annabelle suggested—"Farmer's tan," I pointed out—but at least my T-shirt is a pretty one I've never worn to the barn. My capris still had the tag on them when I pulled them from my drawer. They're far too lightweight and light colored to wear to the barn, but they look great with the T-shirt.

The only thing that's classic me is my feet—my bumpy, calloused, bony feet—but in my sandals, they'll be new to Matt, who's used to seeing me in paddock boots.

Why do I look pretty this time? What makes it different? It's the first time I've looked at my reflection top-to-bottom. All of me at once. Wow, what a difference a little perspective makes. I'd better go before I start zooming in on individual parts and finding reasons to hate them.

Jamie hurtles into my room. "Come on, Gwacie! Matt's downstairs and he's waitin' for you! You wook pwetty enough!"

"Thanks for the subtlety Jay-Jay." I follow him as he runs off again, sliding down the stairs on his bum, leading me to Matt.

◆ ◆ ◆

"You do look pretty," Matt says as he opens the door of the truck for me.

"You, too. But not pretty." Although he's almost perfect enough to be pretty. Almost, but not quite. He's kept just this side of it by virtue of the scar on his chin, a hint of stubble along his jaw line, the cowlick on the crown of his head. Everything just the way I like it.

He takes me to the fair. Which is one hundred percent perfect, with its smells of caramel popcorn, and hay mixed with manure, and diesel from the tractor pull. Music from the midway rides mingles with the ring announcer's booming voice and, in the hall displaying the giant vegetables, the murmur of voices admiring hundred-plus-pound pumpkins and zucchinis grown to the size of a toddler.

Matt holds my hand, and when we see people from school or the barn, he doesn't stop holding it. Every now and then, he gives an extra squeeze to say, "Over this direction" or "Stop a minute and look at this"; riding seems to have given us this language of touch we both understand.

We leave as dark falls, as the lights on the rides flash to life, and the animals are bedded down for the night.

And drive to the field.

I have butterflies, big time.

Because, we're not here to cut grass, and we're not here to watch white clouds scud across a blue summer sky. We're here in the thick dark air of an August evening, with the night sounds of crickets and frogs all around us, with fireflies blinking in the tall grass. I shiver, but not from fear.

"Wait there." Matt pulls a picnic blanket out from behind his seat and hops into the back to spread it out.

"Join me?" he asks through the tiny sliding cab window, and I get out and climb up beside him, and feel like I'm going to be sick to my stomach.

"I ordered a special sunset just for you." He waves out over the field where, at the very far edge, the last intense orange sliver of the sun is slipping down to be swallowed by the distant trees.

"Beautiful." I close my eyes against the nighttime summer breeze fluttering on my cheeks, and when I open them again, I'm looking directly into Matt's eyes. He places his hand over mine and goose bumps run up my arms.

I lean a bit and he leans a bit and, in a minute, our

foreheads are propped together, noses brushing, lips just centimeters apart.

But not for long. Matt's lips touch mine and, despite all the long chapping days outside in the wind and the sun, they're the softest thing I've ever felt. I want to stay like this for ages and feel the softness of his lips while, at exactly the same time, I want to be as close to him as possible, push myself against him, crawl inside his shirt, knock him over backwards.

Matt keeps his hands on mine, steadying me, holding me back so, like a spooked horse, I settle down and focus instead on his teeth lightly gripping my lower lip, then his lips running up the taut line of my neck and stopping somewhere under my earlobe, sending sparks shooting through my brain so stars pop on the inside of my eyelids.

"Happy Birthday, Grace," he whispers in my ear, and I lean into him and we stay there, panting, propping each other up for several long seconds, before he clears his throat and speaks again.

"I swore I wouldn't kiss you until you turned sixteen, and it was worth the wait."

"Thanks a lot. All this time, I thought you didn't like me."

"What's not to like? You're, well, you're intense ..." He holds out his hands to show me, around the base of both palms, tiny crescent-shaped grooves, four on each hand, just where my curling fingers reached up to grip him.

"Me?"

"You."

"Sorry," I say and stare at the blanket, while my cheeks and ears rush hot and red.

"Don't be. I'm glad. I wouldn't have wanted you to be bored."

"Oh, wow. I was so not bored. In fact, is it OK if I show you just how not bored I was?"

And this time, I start the kissing.

When Matt finally drops me off at home, with my skin flushed and my hair mussed, there are a million things running through my mind.

"Does this mean I get to kiss you whenever I want?"

"Definitely," he says. Then laughs. "I mean, you know, within reason."

"In other words, not when Drew's around."

"Probably not."

"OK, so if that's true—about the kissing—how are we ever going to get anything done?"

"Good question. Maybe it's best just to avoid each other."

"Maybe."

"Or maybe not," he says.

And we spend another five minutes kissing before he whispers, "Go, now, quick, before I lose my mind completely."

And as I run for the front door, I think it's a good thing he hasn't lost his mind, because I'm not at all sure mine's intact.

chapter

twenty-nine

I wake up humming. Practice looking at myself—all of myself—in the mirror. Even without the hairstyling of last night, and even in the slouchy tee and yoga shorts I slept in, I look fine.

Don't push it. Move away from the mirror while you're still ok.

I settle on the perfect water temperature in the shower first try, and there's a box of my über-favorite Organic Wheat Squares cereal on the table when I come down for breakfast.

My mouth waters, instantly remembering their sweet nutty taste and how well they soak up the milk. "Where did these come from?!?"

"Can you believe it?" Annabelle says. "They suddenly had them at the grocery store yesterday after how many months?"

"Like, six?" I pour a ridiculously large heap into my bowl, reminiscent of the portion I would have had six months ago, before this all started.

Annabelle hands me an envelope. "I'm sorry. I should have given this to you yesterday. For your birthday. I wanted to, but I couldn't pull it off on time."

I raise my eyebrows. "But you gave me those gorgeous new boots. And the books from Jamie ..." I tear as I talk to reveal a check. A huge check. At least, huge to me.

"It's for Sprite. Put with what you've saved from work this summer, it'll be enough."

"But ..."

She shakes her head. "No buts. I finally talked to your dad yesterday afternoon. He's agreed to hold off on the school."

"He has?"

"Subject to your new therapist's sending him the data from your weigh-ins."

"Whatever! Fine with me! I can't believe it ... but, wait, you *knew* before I went out with Matt?"

"Just. But I didn't want to distract you. I was pretty sure you'd have a good time ..." Her eyebrows are raised, waiting for my response.

I shovel in a heaping spoonful of cereal, mumble around the squares, "It was good."

"That's all?"

I point to my overflowing mouth and shrug.

"Mommy! Mommy!" Jamie's just-woke-up voice drifts down the stairs.

Sometimes I really love that kid.

I cycle off to the barn in a heady, dreamy, happy state, made even happier when Matt sneaks up behind me in the tack room and gives me a kiss on the nape of my neck.

"Oh!" I say—who knew I had that many nerve endings in my neck?—my knees go weak and I whisper, "I thought not around Drew."

"You're right. But I couldn't resist."

"I'm glad."

We stay on track the rest of the day, mostly because we work in separate barns. During the hour we exercise horses in the same ring, Matt calls me over. "I think there's something wrong with your stirrup leather."

"What?" I look down to see what he's doing.

"Nothing," he whispers. "I just wanted to touch you." And he brushes his hand along my leg as he lifts up the loose end of the leather then puts it back in the exact same place.

I spend the rest of my ride acutely aware of a tingling path along the back of my thigh, right where Matt's fingers touched it.

At the end of the day, we say goodbye.

"I've got baseball tonight," he says.

"I know. I'm babysitting Jamie."

"Maybe we can do something tomorrow night?"

I nod. "That would be great. And maybe next time I can come see you play ball?"

"That would be great."

"OK, goodnight."

"Goodnight."

"'Night."

"'Night."

Finally, I swing my leg over my bike. Take one pedal stroke, then another. Look back over my shoulder to catch Matt still watching me. *Keep pedaling.*

At the end of the barn, ride right past Drew, staring back at where Matt and I were standing, where Matt's still waving me off.

"'Night, Drew!" I call cheerfully.

He clears his throat. "Oh, uh, goodnight, Grace. See you tomorrow."

With several trailer loads of horses and riders shipped off to the provincial championships somewhere north of Toronto, Matt and I are taking advantage of our lightened workload to paint the small barn.

He drives his truck right up in front and starts unloading tins of paint and brushes. "You want trim or main color?" he asks. When I hesitate, he decides, "Trim for you," and hands me a slightly narrower brush, indicates the darker paint color. "Go for it."

It alternates between fun, as the first splashes of fresh paint cover the tired old color, and boring as I endlessly, endlessly steady my brush, draw a fine line along the edge of the trim, try not to mar Matt's fresh coat on the walls. Then, when I step back and squint my eyes to see the difference we've made, it's fun again.

My boredom's returning when I step backwards onto a rock, my ankle buckles, and I fall down hard on my backside in the dirt. "Ow!"

Matt, instead of rescuing me, laughs, and I swipe at him with my still-loaded brush. A hunter green stripe slashes across his bare leg.

He stares at it for a minute and I stare at him, half-satisfied, half-horrified by what I've done. He meets my eyes and I think he's going to say something, but, instead, he just lifts his brush and takes a swipe up one of my arms and down the other. The two clay-colored strips are cool on my sun-warmed skin.

I dart forward and dab big green circles on each of his knees and, as I'm scrambling away, his brush tickles the back of my hot neck.

"Whoa!" I grab at my hair for reassurance it's all safely tucked up under my baseball cap.

But I don't have to worry about any more assaults from Matt. He's straightened up and set his brush down.

A gleaming, extremely expensive horse trailer has just rolled quietly into the yard.

"What?" I ask.

A man I've never seen before steps out of the driver's side, and Mavis gets out of the passenger door.

Matt strides forward, hand extended. "You must be Mr.

Stotts. I'm Matt Ancott. Drew asked me to meet you."

The man nods. To his credit, he meets Matt's gaze directly without glancing at his colorful legs. "Call me Lee."

"Lee, this is Grace. She can get Ava while I help you with the trailer. That is, unless you'd rather get her, Mavis."

Mavis yawns. "No, that's fine. It's about time you two did some work for me."

Still unsure what's going on, I head to the main barn, to Ava's big bright stall. She's the only horse left in her aisle. She's already padded up in fluffy white shipping bandages, and her tail's wrapped neatly to protect it in the trailer. Somebody—Matt, I assume—knew she was going and got her ready. *What is up?*

Ava moves beside me sweetly and politely—not lagging behind like most of the school horses; not rushing me like Sprite does—and a pang runs through me. "You are an angel, aren't you?" I stroke her neck as we walk along. She's not a horse I would have chosen, but I'm going to miss her.

When we reach the trailer, Matt and Lee have the ramp down. Lee's inside the trailer, waiting to receive Ava's head, and Matt's standing beside the ramp. Mavis takes two big steps back—my sign to load her horse for her.

"Watch out for her legs, will you, Grace? I know your horse is damaged goods, but that doesn't mean I want mine to be, too."

"Your Mom is a bitch," I coo to Ava, and her pretty ears flick to me, appreciating the soothing sound of my words.

She walks up the ramp smooth as can be, and I hand her lead to Lee and let myself out the side door.

Matt's busy securing the ramp behind Ava, so I grit my teeth and walk over to Mavis. I still don't know why or where, but it's clear she's leaving, so the least I can do is say goodbye. "Well, we've ridden together for a long time, Mavis."

"*Too long* at this dump. At Lee's, we don't have to sweep. They have a proper staff to clean the barn. In fact, I don't even have to groom and tack up if I don't want to."

"I'm sure you'll enjoy that."

"Oh, believe me, I will. It's too bad you can't move to a nice barn, too, Grace but, then again, I don't think your horse would exactly fit in."

I grit my teeth. *She'll be gone soon.* "It sounds perfect for you, Mavis."

To my surprise, Mavis steps forward, puts her bony hands on my shoulders, and gives me her impression of a hug. It's a weak, quick squeeze and, when I try to reciprocate, she feels like a bird under my arms. I'm caught off guard. Maybe all our time riding together has meant something to Mavis. Maybe her mean exterior is just her weird way of showing affection.

She steps back with her eyebrows arched. "So, you've given up on your diet, Grace. Too bad; you were finally making progress."

Matt steps in, puts his arm around my shoulders. "Grace has finally decided to stop hiding how hot she is." He kisses my cheek, and "hot" describes perfectly the flush that spreads across my face. "Glad we could help you get going, Mavis."

Matt helps guide Lee out of the yard and checks his watch. "Time for lunch."

As I swallow a bite of bagel, I shake my head. "I can't believe Mavis would leave here just to avoid having to sweep the aisles. I mean, I can, in a way, but she was winning here with Drew and she's so competitive. I would have thought that would be a big enough incentive to keep her here."

Matt snorts. "Is that what she told you?"

"What do you mean?"

"That she left so she'd get valet service?" He shakes his head. "She left because Drew kicked her out."

"He what? How do you know?"

"I overheard him talking to her in the office. He told her that, in his opinion, she had an eating disorder and needed help. He said if she didn't turn things around, she couldn't show anymore and she'd have to leave. Then, last night, he told me she'd be leaving today and to have Ava ready to go."

The shock is jaw-dropping. Literally. I lean my head against my hand and, with my mouth wide open, struggle to form a coherent sentence. "But ... he never noticed ... he didn't know ..."

Matt laughs. "Grace, do you really think Drew didn't notice? When has Drew ever not noticed anything?"

"But he never said."

"He was watching you. God, Grace, we were all watching

you. *Karen's* been watching you. Even Kelly's been watching you."

"So, Drew cared?"

"Of course he cared. We all cared. We all wanted you to get better, and we all thought you might be just that bit smarter than Mavis. That you might actually get your shit together and sort things out."

"Well, he's got a funny way of showing he cares."

"We're talking about Drew, right? How long have you known him and you're still surprised he has a funny way of doing things?"

It hits me that Matt's right. There have been lots of times I knew Drew was paying attention; I just assumed the worst, thought he was being critical instead of caring. I drop my gaze, study a dent in the top of the picnic table. "I feel stupid."

Matt reaches out, cups my chin, lifts my eyes to his. "You're not stupid. You're very, very cute. Speaking of which, what are you doing tonight?"

I let my chin rest in his warm hand and half-close my eyes. "Um, watching a baseball game, maybe?"

"Oh, yeah?"

"And then seeing a movie with the center fielder?"

"Sold."

chapter

thirty-one

"**N**umber twenty-seven, you're on deck!" the whipper-in calls.

"You ready?" I smooth a gloved hand down Sprite's gleaming neck.

"He's ready," Matt says. "And so are you."

"I hope you're right."

We both wince as the hollow racket of jump rails hitting first each other, then the ground, rings through the air. I turn around in my saddle to watch the horse on course tiptoe his way out of the mess of pick-up-sticks he's made of the third jump.

"Nobody's gone clear, yet," Matt says. "That's all you have to do to win."

"Oh, is that it?" I give him an overly sweet smile. "Thanks so much."

I ride by Drew on my way in. "All you have to do is go clear," he says. I liked it better when Matt was saying it.

I shorten my reins an inch, squeeze Sprite forward into the ring, "All you have to do is go clear," I stage whisper at him. His ears flick back for half a second, then swivel around to where the final reconstruction touches are being put on jump three.

I take him into a sweeping trot. Lovely, rounded, ground-eating. He holds the bit like it was china and I give his mouth the same respect. All my aids are at 0.5, barely there. I wonder how long that'll last.

Ask for the canter and receive a perfect one. Collected and smooth; pretty to look at, dreamy to sit.

Something's wrong, though. There's a feeling in my bones I normally get, especially on Sprite, at the beginning of a course. It's not with me today.

He's been much better since his injury. Such a nicer horse. "Nearly safe to handle," Andy said last night, as he stood unusually quiet for his braiding.

But he's not Sprite. Not the horse I signed up to lease at the beginning of the summer. I've lost a lot and gained a lot this summer. Some of the losses were even good, but not this one. I miss my bad boy.

We're in our approach circle to the first fence, cantering pleasantly along the fence line, when a woman coming down from the stands trips. "Oh!" She tips forward and throws out her hand just in time to catch the fence, stop herself from falling.

Sprite pins his ears back, gives a sideways snatch at the bit and lets out an almighty buck. There's a gasp behind me, and I even think I can hear the woman calling, "Sorry!" but I don't care.

"We're going to kill this course!" I tell Sprite. He yanks hard on my hands and bears down on the first jump like a runaway train.

Because he's running and not listening to me, he's not set up right for the jump. We're either going to dig in too close to the base, or we'll have to take off from a ridiculously far spot. I close my legs on him, sink my heels low, and concentrate on just letting him jump. He explodes from nearly a length out, heaves himself up with a huge grunt and, despite my preparations, pops me six inches out of the saddle. We clear the jump by a foot.

There's my fighter. I decide, as much as possible, to just let him go. I'll intervene only if we're at serious risk of physical harm.

He clears two and three as though they were ground poles. He gives a little tail flick as he soars over three, as if to say, "I'm sorry, but is there something difficult about this jump?"

Jump four is big, and all by itself, and there's a sharp turn to five. I turn Sprite in the air over four so he lands on the right arc for five, then sit down on his back and half-halt. Hard. He inverts his neck, throws his head in the air, keeps running. Half-halt again. Harder. And one more for good measure.

I can almost hear him say it: Oh, OK, as he slackens his pace, tucks his hocks underneath him, and agrees to cover the distance to the jump in six more strides, instead of the five he had in mind.

It's a beautiful jump; his neck and body arch in a fantastic bascule but, being Sprite, he can't resist throwing in a buck on the far side.

I evaluate the remaining jumps, conclude there's nothing Sprite can't handle, and lean forward, rubbing his neck. "It's all yours, boy." His ears flick back, then forward, and he up-shifts. More speed, more power, more fun.

He's full of fight. But not with me. Just with the jumps. I steer and he runs and, together, we have the most fun I've ever experienced finishing a course.

It's stride, stride, stride, leap, fly, land, and dig in again to stride, stride, stride.

And then it's over. I'm elated and deflated. Wish we could do it again. Realize we can, just not immediately. "Good boy," I tell the still-running Sprite. "We're done."

He lowers his head, stretches out his neck, and slows to a reasonable canter to carry me safely back to the gate.

Photo Credit: Debora Dekok

Interview with Tudor Robins

Tudor, you are with a horse in your author photo. Who is this horse?

The horse in the photo is Abercrombie. He's an off-the-track thoroughbred who lives at Meadowvale Farm (www.meadowvalefarm.ca) near Carp, Ontario.

Crombie has a massive personality. He's very tactile and seems to always be doing something with his mouth, whether it's trying to nibble on his cross-ties, or curling his lip up in the air, or—his favorite—eating carrots. The first time I met him, he was lying in his stall, snoring *very* loudly. He's not a boring horse.

He also loves to jump and, at least once in every ride, will jump twice as high as he needs to. He's got quite a motor and, while I loved riding him right away, it took a while for us to understand one another so we could find a speed we both agreed on.

I'm very lucky to be able to ride such a great horse, and I'm constantly grateful to Stephanie Calvert, who owns both Abercrombie and Meadowvale, for letting me ride him.

How long have you been riding?

I took my first lunge line lesson when I was eight years old. This means I've been riding for over thirty years!

What do you love best about riding?

It's very hard to choose one thing I love most about riding. I love everything about being around horses. I love being in the country. I love the kind of people who ride. I love that you can never, ever, know all there is to know about horses and taking care of them and riding them. I do *adore* jumping. Most of all, though, if I had to pick one thing, I'd say I love how, when I ride, I forget about *everything else in the world*. I really do. From the moment I mount up, until my instructor says, "I think that's enough," I don't think about anything except bending and flexing and rhythm, and it's always a shock to come back to the real world. So, for me, riding is a vacation I'm lucky to be able to take one night every week.

Of all the horses you've cared for, do you have a favorite?

At every point in my riding career, I have always had a favorite horse. While I enjoy riding in general, what makes it particularly rewarding is to have a favorite to focus on. Right now, Abercrombie is it. I literally took one look at him, the first time I ever walked into the barn at Meadowvale, and thought, "I hope I get to ride that horse."

However, for the purposes of this question, the most interesting "favorite" is probably a small quarter horse(ish) mare named Lass. She was smaller than most horses I ride and she was a liver chestnut—not usually my favorite color—and, yes, she had been badly neglected to the point of starvation. She was not Whinny—not exactly—but she inspired Whinny.

I knew Lass many, many years ago now, but I will always remember her, and it's wonderful to know she recovered fully so that many other riders would be able to also have her as a favorite over the years.

You've done a lot of writing for magazines and newspapers. What made you decide to write a novel?

Writing a novel has always been my dream, but it's a big, daunting, challenging dream and, for a long time, I didn't know how to go about it.

Going to journalism school was a big step, and I'm glad I did because I learned so much about writing, interviewing, researching, and just generally being tenacious. However, journalism school prepares you to be a journalist, so I learned how to write for newspapers and magazines, and did that for quite a while.

When I had my children, everything changed. I looked at my priorities and made hard decisions about how to spend my time, and part of that was realizing I had to finally finish a novel and work hard at getting it published.

What do you love best about writing?

I can't not write. It's as simple as that. You know that feeling you get when you're in the middle of a great book, and you're just itching to finish your chores or your homework so you can get back to it? That's how I feel about writing.

I used to finish a great novel and think, "I wish I could read something else that would make me feel that way." Now, when I write, I'm trying to write that novel—the next book I'd want to read.

Readers often wonder if the main character of a novel is really the author in disguise. Are there aspects of your life and/or personality that made their way into the creation of Grace?

The way I've grown up, the things I've learned, and the life I've lived have definitely shaped the way I've written this story. However, I am not Grace and Grace is not me. As I wrote this story, Grace grew in my heart and in my mind. There are things I knew Grace would do and things I knew Grace wouldn't do. I didn't decide these things; I just knew them, somehow.

Grace has many advantages I didn't have at her age. I think she's smarter and stronger than I was. She gets to ride much more than I did at fifteen-turning-sixteen, and she's a better rider than I was at that age. Finally—and unfortunately for me—I did *not* have a Matt when I was Grace's age!

I think it's important to say, I have experienced an eating disorder. I began showing signs of anorexia when I was ten years old, and it flared up again when I was about twenty and at university. My belief is that, like other people who have been anorexic and "recovered," I will always see the world a little differently. Even if I don't still have all the same feelings and compulsions I did at those times, I still remember them and I understand them. I hope this has helped me write a sympathetic account of Grace's experiences.

How typical do you think Grace is of girls with anorexia?

There are some things that are generally considered "typical" of girls with anorexia, and Grace displays some of those. For example, an obsession with weighing herself, detailed calorie-counting, a distorted view of her own size, and other such traits. However, beyond those common realities of anorexia, I think most people experience the condition quite differently. Some girls (and boys—they can have eating disorders, too!) get really, very ill and will never truly recover and, tragically, some die. Some anorexia sufferers require hospitalization, while others don't.

This story is not meant to show "how anorexia progresses" but rather how a specific character—Grace—experiences her anorexia. She doesn't represent all anorexics but, in some ways, at some times, I think most anorexics will find something they recognize in Grace's story.

Do you have any advice for readers who have issues around eating or body image, or who might be concerned about someone they suspect might have an eating disorder?

We're all insecure about our looks sometimes, but if it starts affecting our health, our relationships, or the way we carry out our day-to-day activities, it's time to talk to somebody and ask for help.

If you have a trusted family doctor, that's a great resource. You can also turn to the National Eating Disorder Information Centre (NEDIC) at 1-866-NEDIC-20 (1-866-633-

4220) or www.nedic.ca to get help for yourself, or to find out how to help somebody you know.

NEDIC has a poster that says, "Talking Saves Lives," and I agree with this a hundred percent.

Any advice for girls who want to excel at riding? Or at writing?

It's essential to enjoy the process—both in riding and writing. There is joy at each level of achievement and accomplishment and, as Grace discovered during her summer, there are different ways to be successful in what you're doing.

Both riding and writing are great because they offer near-endless opportunities. You can ride English or Western. You can do dressage or hunter-jumper, or learn to play polo or become an endurance rider.

Writing is the same. You can write poetry, short stories, novellas, and novels. You can write for many different age groups in a wide variety of genres and categories.

Best of all, neither riding nor writing has an age limit, so you have your whole life to improve and enjoy them.

What would you rather be doing: riding or writing?

I write much more often than I ride. I write pretty much every day, and I definitely feel "itchy" if one or two days go by when I don't have a chance to write.

Although I don't feel the need to ride daily, it is important to me to ride regularly—once a week seems about right for me. The things I do other than writing—like riding, running, and skiing—let the writing part of my brain rest so that, often, I have great ideas when I get back to writing.